2.95/N

The Whale People

The
Whale People

RODERICK HAIG-BROWN

DRAWINGS BY MARY WEILER

COLLINS

LONDON & TORONTO

© Roderick Haig-Brown, 1962
Printed in Great Britain by
Collins Clear-Type Press: London and Glasgow

CONTENTS

Contents

To
the Indian Peoples
of the Northern Pacific

ACKNOWLEDGMENT

The author wishes gratefully to acknowledge the immense assistance he has received from the following sources:

CURTIS, EDWARD S.
The Nootka, Vol. XI, "The North American Indian". 1916.

DRUCKER, PHILIP
The Northern and Central Nootkan Tribes. Bureau of American Ethnology, Bulletin 144. 1951.

DENSMORE, FRANCES
Nootka and Quileute Music. Bureau of American Ethnology, Bulletin 124. 1939.

WATERMAN, T. T.
The Whaling Equipment of the Makah Indians University of Washington, Anthropology, Vol. I, No. 1, 1920. Reprinted 1955.

Without the guidance of these scientific works, rich in detail, it would not have been possible to write the book at all. For all sins of projection and imagination herein committed the present author takes full responsibility.

RODERICK HAIG-BROWN
Campbell River, B.C.
4 December, 1961

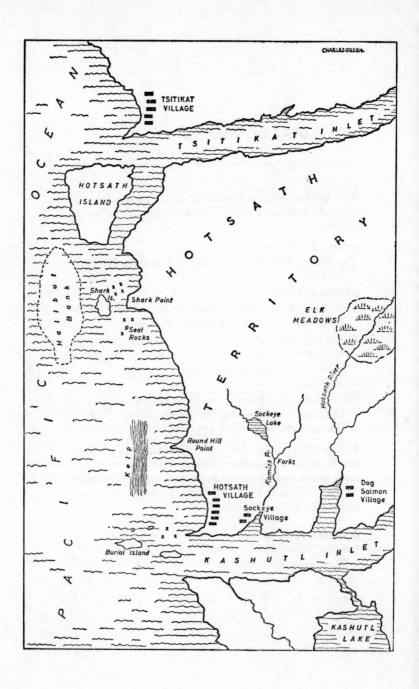

1. *The Salmon*

It was a hot day, with a westerly wind, but inside Kashutl Inlet, behind the rock bluffs of the northern shore, the water was still as glass. The two boys, Atlin and Hinak, were letting the canoe drift over the cod-bank that lay a few hundred feet out from the bluffs. The canoe tilted far over as both boys gazed down into the still water. They could not see the bottom, even in the strong sunlight that streamed past them into the water, but the water itself was alive with the drift and movement of millions of tiny creatures and the flash of the eel-like bodies of the needlefish. The boys gazed past all this, into the deeper invisible depths from which they hoped to draw another movement.

Hinak, a tall slender boy of fourteen, was pushing a long pole rather carefully down into the water, hand over hand. Atlin, who was shorter, more heavily built and some two years younger, was holding another pole in a thrusting position, but his eyes were on the distorted length of Hinak's pole as it pushed down into the depths. The pole in Atlin's hands was an old two-headed salmon spear of his father's, with points of bone and horn set in sockets at the tip and secured to the shaft by short lines of nettle fibre. Although he was the younger of the two, it was Atlin and not Hinak who held the spear and made all the final decisions. He was the chief's son. Hinak was the son of a slave from a distant tribe, taken in war many years earlier.

Hinak's hands reached the end of his long pole and he held it for a moment, resisting the lift of the water. Then he thrust down hard and pulled sharply back almost in the same movement. The pole leapt through his hands until he caught it again at the point of balance and swung it behind him into the canoe. All the while he kept his eyes on the deep water under the canoe, as did Atlin. Very soon they saw what they were looking for, the twinkling flashes of the lure released from the tip of Hinak's pole. It was nothing more than a round piece of white wood, shaped and tapered to the form of a small fish and fitted with two thin blades of wood that made it spin as it rose through the water. It came up slowly, veering a little away from the canoe, gradually revealing its true shape and size. Both boys watched in utter absorption. Then suddenly the fish was there, close to it, rising with it, a great, broad-mouthed ling cod lifting its shadowy body at exactly the same speed as the lure. Atlin's body tensed slightly. He could see the line of the closed mouth and the blank, emotionless stare of the eyes. The fish seemed to be coming more slowly than the lure now and he knew it could stop suddenly and sink back into the depths as effortlessly as it had risen from them, but he waited. The lure wobbled the last few feet and broke the surface, the fish moved and Atlin struck. It was a good thrust and the leading point drove in just behind the gill-covers, burying the horn barbs of the point in the flesh. The fish threshed at the surface, but Atlin drew back his pole, hand over hand, until Hinak reached out, seized the nettle-cord and heaved the fish aboard.

"It was a good strike, Chief," he said to the younger boy. "I think it is the big one that would not come up far enough before."

Atlin squatted in the canoe, cutting his point and barbs out of the fish. It was by far the largest of the dozen or more on the bottom of the canoe, but he said: "I'm tired of these old cod. Catching them is woman's work."

"It is better than playing on the beach," Hinak said. "When he sees the fish perhaps your grandfather will believe you are strong enough to hunt seals."

"He will say it is not time. He will say a man needs strong spirit help to hunt seals and whales."

"That is true," agreed Hinak. "But your father, Nit-gass, has shown you many things already."

Both boys glanced up as a bald eagle came gliding towards them from his watching place in a tall tree on the shore line. He passed low over the canoe, carried on for two or three hundred yards, then dipped to brush the water and came up with several small fish in his claws.

"Herring," said Atlin excitedly. "Right at the surface." He had picked up a paddle and was already swinging the canoe from the stern. Hinak moved swiftly to the bow with his own paddle and together they drove the canoe with silent strokes to where the eagle had made his catch. Just short of the faint ripples that were still spreading, Hinak put down his paddle and picked up a long flat lath of wood, set with sharp bone teeth at one end, like a rake. Holding this ready in his hands he peered over the prow of the canoe, while Atlin slowed their swift movement. Suddenly Hinak plunged the toothed end of his rake into the water, edge first, and swept it back, then up and out of the water with several bright little fish wriggling on the bone teeth. He shook them off into the canoe, raked again, shook off a single fish and raked yet again. Altogether he raked about a dozen times and brought in twenty or thirty herring. Then he said: "They've gone down."

"It's enough," said Atlin. "Will there be salmon?"

"Yes," said Hinak confidently, "or the herring would not be so high up in the water."

As he spoke a shower of little fish broke the surface forty or fifty yards away and the swirl of a big fish feeding showed near them. Atlin reached under a damp cedar bark mat and brought out a coil of stretched kelp line. Hinak picked up two of the herrings and came quickly back to the stern. From a cedar box he took a nettle-cord leader with a sharp angled hook attached to it. The hook was barbless, a sharp bone point securely lashed to a piece of spruce root. While Atlin watched him, Hinak took a slender piece of bone, notched at one end, and pushed the leader through the herring's vent and out at its mouth. Then he slid the herring down very carefully until it was lodged firmly in the angle of the hook. Both boys were very excited and Atlin kept glancing up to look for more signs of feeding salmon.

"Shall we catch one, do you think?" he asked. "Tetacus,

14

my grandfather, says the salmon only come up to feed like this when it is nearly dark, or in the early morning."

"They are feeding now," Hinak said. "We can try." He had pierced the upper and lower jaws of the herring and was tying its mouth shut with a short piece of fibre. "You have salmon power because you are the son and grandson of chiefs. If you hold the line they will come to the hook."

Atlin picked up his paddle and began to move the canoe, smoothly and easily, towards the last place they had seen a fish break. Hinak put the baited hook overboard and watched the herring as it gleamed and turned to the pressure of the water. He paid out fifteen or twenty feet of line, then gave it to Atlin, who held it between his right hand and the paddle. Hinak picked up his own paddle.

A feeding salmon swirled directly ahead of them and the canoe bow glided silently into the ripples of its movement. Atlin glanced over his shoulder at the herring trailing behind him. Each time he moved his hand forward to make a new stroke with the paddle he could see the glint of the little fish close under the surface. It sank back with the stroke, to dart forward again as the paddle lifted.

The strike was so sudden and powerful that it forced his arm back and tore the line through his grip. He swung the paddle sharply inboard with his left hand, turned and got both hands on the line. The fish was threshing violently at the surface so that they could see the breadth of his silver side in the churning water. In spite of himself Atlin gave a little more line, then held firmly as the fish began to tow the canoe stern first. It had worked down now and the kelp line throbbed with the power of its movement, cutting the surface of the water like a tiny canoe prow. Then the fish was straight down, under the canoe.

Both boys were in the stern, peering over into the sunlit water. Atlin held until the sweat started on his face and chest.

From far below, the fish's frantically twisting body sent its flashes through the lightly rippled water. "It is a king of salmon," said Hinak. "As big as a little whale."

"All the village will come out to see him," said Atlin. "As they come for my father when he brings a whale to the beach. But it would be better if we had a whale line to hold him."

Suddenly the pull on the line changed, becoming lighter at first, then vibratingly strong as the big fish swam up for the surface. He burst out in the sunlight only twenty or thirty feet away, huge and magnificent, crashed back on his side, broke again. The line slid through Atlin's unwilling hands and he glanced anxiously at the few coils left in the bottom of the canoe. The canoe was moving through the water now, easing the strain, but the fish kept the line so tight that Atlin could feel the throb and flutter of his tail against it. Then the fish jumped again, high out of the water, and the drag of the line threw him over in a somersault. The hook tore away and the line went slack.

Hinak heaved a great sigh of disappointment. Atlin uttered a growling sound and pounded his fist on the gunwale.

"He was too strong," Hinak said. "He was the big chief of all the salmon."

"It is true he was strong," agreed Atlin. "But it is more true we were not ready for him. If we had tied a seal bladder to the line he would not have got away."

"We did not have one," said Hinak. He was examining the hook Atlin had recovered. The herring was gone, but otherwise it was unharmed.

"We could have brought one. Next time we will. Put on another herring, quickly."

They went back to fishing, but it seemed that the feeding flurry was over. No more salmon swirled and no herring jumped or showed. Atlin's eagerness faded and he began to think of other things. His father, Nit-gass, the principal chief of the Hotsath Indian people, had left on a whaling expedition two days earlier. It was likely he would come back that evening or at least that there would be news of him. The same thought came to Hinak at about the same time.

"Your father will bring his whale to the village tonight," he said.

"If he has killed a whale," said Atlin, "and if the whale has swum towards the shore and not out to sea."

"It is a good time for the whales. I heard your uncle, Tokwit, say there are many, close in to shore. When your father strikes a whale the harpoon goes to the whale's heart."

"Not always," said Atlin. "The whale that broke his canoe last year was not struck to the heart."

"But Chief Nit-gass killed him and brought him to the beach. Last year he brought in more whales than any chief before him. He is the greatest of all the whale chiefs."

"That is true," said Atlin. "He will bring a whale tonight. But it is not good to say it too soon. My mother says the whale is more powerful than any man, even my father, and no man can say what he will do before it is done."

Hinak accepted the reproof. "If there is a whale on the beach tonight, your father will want you to stand with him when he divides it among the people."

"I do not care for that," said Atlin shortly.

"It is an honour."

"It would be better to go out in the whale canoe. Why does he not take me?"

"Perhaps it will be soon," said Hinak.

"He was no older than me when Tetacus first took him. I know that. He has told me himself." Atlin put down his paddle and began to coil the kelp trolling line. "One day I shall be a whaling chief and you can be my steersman. Then we will kill whales every day."

"I am the son of a slave," Hinak reminded him.

17

"You are also my brother," said Atlin, turning the canoe as he spoke. "Where I go, you must go. My father has ordered it. When I am the whale chief, I shall order it."

"I believe you, Chief," said Hinak gently. "But all this will not be tomorrow."

Atlin laughed, his moment of dignity betrayed. "No," he said. "We have not learned to catch a salmon yet." They met the afternoon breeze as they came towards the mouth of the inlet and the canoe began to dance against the whitecaps. Soon they would be rounding the point in the partial shelter of Burial Island and the rocky islets near it, then they would be in sight of the Hotsath village beach and whatever was going on there.

2. The Whale

As SOON as the boys rounded the point they saw that the whale was already on the beach and had been for some time. The people of the village were still crowded around the whale; Nit-gass and his steersman Tokwit stood a little apart, watching attentively. But the heavy work of stripping the blubber was already far advanced and great slabs of it lay on the beach, each assigned to its rightful owner.

Atlin knew every stage of the process, for he had watched it many times. The humped saddle of the whale had been cut away at once and carried up to a place just behind his father's house, where it would be hung on a strong pole and decorated with dyed cedar bark and eagle feathers. Next the harpoon heads had been cut out, carefully cleaned and stowed away. While this was going on other men had staked the whale securely down to the beach so that no sudden storm could carry it away. Then Nit-gass and Tokwit, his steersman and speaker, had withdrawn to where they now stood; Nit-gass had assigned special cuts of the whale—the tongue, the flippers, strips of the belly—to those who had helped him, speaking through Tokwit.

The boys brought the canoe in quietly through the light surf and Atlin went at once to his father. Because he knew it was a ceremonial occasion, he said nothing but simply stood to the right of Nit-gass and a little behind him. Nit-gass continued to watch the excited people working on the whale carcass. Occasionally he said something to Tokwit, who limped forward and repeated it, speaking loudly to be heard above the talk and laughter. Nit-gass' black bear robe was thrown down beside him on the sand and both men were naked except for their whaler's hats of tightly woven spruce roots. Nit-gass was very dark, a short, broadchested man, heavily muscled, his skin gleaming with health. Tokwit, too, was a powerful man, with a deep chest and mighty shoulders, but his left leg was twisted and wasted so that he limped heavily and looked always lopsided. Beside these two, Atlin felt very small and unimportant. He wondered how he could ever have talked with Hinak of killing seals and whales.

After a little while Nit-gass half turned, set his right hand on his son's shoulder and drew him gently beside him. With his left hand he still held a pad of shredded cedar bark over his mouth and nostrils. Atlin knew that this was because he was not supposed to smell the whale carcass. Though the whaling chief owned the whales he harpooned and brought to the village beaches, he must never eat any of the blubber or meat, nor smell too deeply of the whale's carcass nor take any direct part in the butchering once he had cut away the saddle which was his own share. Even the saddle must be given away after he and his wife had decorated and danced before it on four successive nights. If he failed in any of these things, his whale spirit would be offended and would reduce the power it gave him.

"Where have you been, Chief?" Nit-gass asked. "I thought you would be here waiting for me when I brought my whale to the beach."

"We were fishing in the Inlet, Hawil," said Atlin.

"Your Mother says you are out all the time since your grandfather gave you the canoe."

The Whale

"Hinak was with me, Hawil . . . We did not go far."

"I did not mean you should stay home," said Nit-gass. "It is good to go out on the water. That is where you learn things, eh, Tokwit?"

Tokwit nodded, his attention still on the whale carcass. "A whale chief's son must go out on the water. He will not learn on the beaches."

"What did you catch, boy?" asked Nit-gass.

"Only the cultus cod. But we hooked a great salmon that was chasing the herrings and he broke away."

"In the Inlet?" Nit-gass was surprised. "On the surface? How big a fish was it?"

Atlin looked at his father with troubled eyes. He could find no way to express the greatness of the fish. "He was very great," he said at last. "Longer than a canoe paddle and twice as wide as the blade. I could not hold him with the line. Hinak will tell you."

"A big spring salmon," said Nit-gass. "It is early. We must tell the people to watch for them. You did well."

"But he broke away. And a salmon is not like a whale or a seal."

Nit-gass laughed. "A salmon as long as a canoe paddle, on a hook, is big enough," he said. "Especially when you are not very big yourself. What shall I tell him, Tokwit?"

Tokwit grinned. "Tell him you said this whale is too little. It is not only the young ones that are hard to satisfy."

"It is true," said Nit-gass. "He is only Ma-ak, the grey whale. And he is little, as you know."

"Ma-ak has broken many canoes," said Tokwit. "And taken many good whalers down into the sea with him."

Atlin listened in fascination to this argument between his father and his father's uncle, the two men he admired most in all the world. Nit-gass spoke impatiently. "We have killed many such whales, you and I. Yet each time it must be made to seem a great thing. We must stand here and divide it so that each man has his proper share. They know the shares as well as we do."

"It is important," said Tokwit simply. "If the Chief was not there to tell them there would be quarrelling."

Nit-gass laughed scornfully. "The old men would swear and scold a little. No one would be hurt. Instead of this we could be hunting more whales."

Tokwit glanced at Atlin, to make sure he was listening. "There is a time for everything, Hawil," he said, using the whale chief's title. "Time to make the people happy, time to get ready for the whale, time to hunt the whale. It is not good to hurry. When the whale chief hurries the harpoon does not go home."

There was a sudden commotion among the men working on the whale, some angry talk, laughter and more talk. A man had been cut quite severely by a slip of one of the sharp shell knives. Nit-gass, watching closely, spoke a few words to Tokwit. Tokwit laughed and stepped forward.

"The Chief says the little whale is more dangerous dead than alive. He is such a little whale he will be afraid and go back to sea if you quarrel and make all that noise."

Everybody laughed and several voices urged the cutters to get back to their work. The wounded man checked his bleeding with a pad of cedar bark and began to ply his knife again. Nit-gass took up his discussion with Tokwit as though nothing had happened.

"It is time for a big whale," he said. "Not Ma-ak. No Soreface. Perhaps Tsi-tsi-cwun, the blue whale, perhaps Kot-ske the sperm whale himself, with his great head full of oil."

Tokwit knew what this meant. Nit-gass loved the excitements and dangers of whaling as he loved nothing else in the world. Now, like all really successful whaling chiefs, he wanted newer and greater excitements, triumphs that would make his name forever great among his people.

"It is not good to despise Ma-ak and the Sorefaces," he said gravely. "If they are offended they can break a canoe and kill us all as quickly as Kot-ske or Tsi-tsi-cwun. Besides, there are other things to be done."

Nit-gass laughed the big deep laugh that Atlin loved to hear. "I do not despise them. I love them as my brothers. That is why they take my harpoon and swim quietly to the beach with it. What other things are there?"

Tokwit pointed to Atlin. "There is the young chief. It will soon be time for him to come with us."

Nit-gass turned at once to his son, looking at him as though for the first time. "Is that true, Chief?" he asked. "Are you ready to go with us to hunt whales?" He held the boy off from him, both hands on his shoulders.

Atlin felt his heart jump in his chest and struggled to find words to answer. "If you will take me, Hawil," he said at last.

Nit-gass lifted him like a feather and set him on his feet again beside Tokwit. "Of course he is ready. Wait till you see it, Chief, when Tokwit puts me so close to him you could reach out and touch his side. That will make the blood jump all through you."

"You will take him to the shrine at the Forks first?" Tokwit asked. It was more nearly a statement than a question.

Nit-gass nodded. "He has been bathing since the herring month. He is ready for that too."

"But he is not ready for Kot-ske," said Tokwit grimly.

Nit-gass laughed his big laugh again. He was very happy. "Not yet, perhaps. But one day. You will see."

3. *The Shrine*

WHEN NIT-GASS woke Atlin to take him to the shrine, it was still completely dark. Atlin woke easily to the touch of his father's hand on his shoulder, as he had on many other mornings. He said: "Yes, father," pushed back the cedar bark mat that covered him and swung his bare legs over the edge of his bench-like bed in the smoky gloom of the great house. The fires in the centre of the house had died down to glowing red embers that would soon be stirred back to life again in the new day, but they gave light enough for him to see his father's form and he waited for the half-joking words that would tell him to go down to the water: "Hurry, boy, before the water is awake. It is not so cold then."

But his father said instead: "It will be daylight very soon and we have a long way to go." Then Atlin remembered that this was the day they were to go to the shrine. He got up and followed his father through the long house, between the families sleeping on either side of it, and out through the small door at the front that opened on to the beach.

They took an old sealing canoe of his father's and ran it down the beach to the edge of the gently heaving sea, launched it and jumped in. As Atlin picked up his paddle in the bow he felt the strong drive of his father's first thrust behind him.

24

The Shrine

A sea mist hid the stars, but the light of the young moon somewhere above it filtered through. The canoe turned along the gentle swells and Atlin knew they had swung south, towards Kashutl Inlet. It was the first time he had been alone in a canoe with his father and he was proud and glad, but at the same time a little afraid. He knew that this was another step towards becoming a man and he wondered if he would be ready for it. Then he remembered what Tetacus had told him about being afraid: "All men are afraid sometimes. It may be good or it may be bad. When you are afraid, ask yourself why. If there is something to be done to make you safer, do it. If there is nothing to be done, then do not bother with fear. It is no help." Atlin knew he was afraid of what he did not know, of what he might see and how he might be tested and whether he would be ready. He thought it might be good to stay a little afraid so that he would be ready.

They had turned into Kashutl Inlet now. Somewhere in the mist there was the sigh of a porpoise surfacing, then from the other side the harsh call of a heron coming to his feeding before the dawn.

Nit-gass said: "The salmon will feed again this morning."

"Could we catch one?" Atlin asked.

"It would be good if we could. But there are other things to do."

"Afterwards?"

"It will be too late, I expect."

Again Atlin wondered just what it was they were going to do. It was four days and four nights since Tokwit had warned his father of the need to take him to the shrine before he went out in the whaling canoe. Atlin had recognised the warning in his great uncle's tone, even though he had not understood it as fully as had Nit-gass. It had meant that Atlin must be made fit to go out with the other men, prepared by some ceremony or experience that would satisfy the whale spirit. It meant that the bathing he had done since early spring—going out in the cold dawns to plunge into the icy water and crouch there until he could stand it no longer—was not enough. A whaler, he knew, learned to swim like a whale, slowly and smoothly, now blowing, now diving, in the same rhythms as the whaler's dances. His mother had told him this many times. A whaler had special prayers and songs after bathing; he rubbed himself with bundles of hemlock branches and nettles until his body was raw and bleeding; he learned to go without food and without sleep so that the spirits would come to him more readily. These things were hard enough, but Atlin thought he could learn them all if he had to. It was the other things that troubled him—the things he had heard from the young men and boys of the village as they played and talked on the beaches.

The mist had lifted a little from the water now and he could see that they were coming in towards the mouth of Kamiss River, the stream up which the sockeye salmon ran to Kamiss Lake. He heard his father set down his paddle and pick up the pole and soon the swift, broken water of the little river was all about them. He kept paddling steadily in the bow, as he had been taught to, hearing the grate of his father's pole against the rocky bottom and feeling the great thrust of his arms as the canoe leapt forward against the current. At one moment a rock would be breaking white in a roar of water beside them, in the next it would be astern and another would be looming ahead. In the excitement of travelling upstream through the semi-darkness Atlin almost forgot his worries about the skulls and skeletons and newly dead corpses that whalers were said to use in seeking the favour of the whale spirit.

Nit-gass had no idea of his son's anxiety. He was enjoying the early morning, the smooth, powerful thrust of his muscles and the easy glide of the canoe against the heavy water. He liked the way Atlin accepted the duty ahead of him, without asking useless questions and without sign of doubt or fear. He admired his son's easy poise in the bow of the canoe and his quiet, steady paddling that made ready allowances for the current changes and the thrust of the pole. So far he had given little thought to what he would do or what he would tell Atlin when they came to the shrine and the bathing pool at the Forks of the river. He was so used to the loyalty of his whaling crew and his own complete authority that Tokwit's warning had surprised him a little. Yet he had known instantly that Tokwit was right. All whaling crews believed that they could succeed in the superhuman task of killing a whale only through the spirit power that came to them through their own, and especially through their chief's, careful performance of ceremonial rites. Any failure or accident, any unusual difficulty would be blamed on a lack of spirit power. Even a passenger, though he was the son and grandson of whaling chiefs and would one day be a whaling chief himself, must have made his peace with the whale spirit or the crew's confidence might be lessened; and confidence, Nit-gass well knew, was the real secret of success in striking and killing whales.

He could hear the sound of the falls where the east fork came into the main stream. He thrust again with his pole and the canoe slid out on to the smooth surface of the big pool at the Forks, where he had bathed regularly ever since he was a boy of Atlin's age. There was some daylight now through the mist that clung to the treetops, but the sun had not risen. He beached the canoe on the east side of the pool because the other side was a sheer rock wall, and climbed out as Atlin held it.

"We will go to the shrine first, Chief," he told his son. "Can you swim across? We have to go close to the falls, but it is easy."

Atlin looked at the white glint of foam below the falls and

the water racing away from it, but he saw the distance was quite short. "Yes," he said. "I can swim there."

"Come on then," Nit-gass told him. "I will be close to you." He dropped his bear robe on the gravel beach and plunged into the water. Atlin followed closely, gasping at the coldness of the water on his chest and belly. He saw his father's head in front of him; then Nit-gass circled and came below him. Together they crossed the main stream and felt bottom under their feet in the eddy between the two currents.

"Go first," Nit-gass said. "Keep close to the falls. Don't be afraid of them."

Atlin pushed out into the foaming water. The sound of the falls thundered in his ears and bubbles leapt in his face, but he could feel the surge of water lifting him and a moment later he was clambering out on to a great rock on the far side. His father came out and sat beside him.

"It was easy, wasn't it?" Nit-gass said.

"Yes, but it was cold."

"The water comes from the snow on the high mountains," said Nit-gass. "It is very cold and very clean." He stood up. "It is only a little way to the shrine from here."

They began to climb and Atlin saw that they were making their way up an enormous pile of moss-covered rocks that sloped up the hillside. It grew lighter as they climbed, though the mist was still quite thick all about them. Nit-gass turned suddenly to his left and they came out on to a flat, grassy place with a high rock bluff at one side of it. A long sloping roof of cedar boards, supported by heavy posts, stood against it and Atlin knew that this was his father's shrine.

Nit-gass went at once to the shrine and Atlin followed, but hesitated at the entrance.

"Come inside," Nit-gass said. "It is a sacred place, but you are the whale chief's son."

Still hesitantly, Atlin came round the first post and under

28

the roof. The walls at the end and on the outer side were quite low, so that a good deal of light came in through the space between them and the sloping roof, but it was still the vague light that comes before sunrise and at first Atlin could not make out anything very clearly. A number of carved wooden figures of men were propped against the outside wall. The broken pieces of a harpoon shaft slanted against the rock. At the far end of the shrine was a carved wooden model of a whale with a huge square head, quite unlike any whale Atlin had ever seen, with a harpooneer standing in the model of a canoe, his harpoon poised, behind it. Running down the centre of the shrine was a rack on which hung many bundles of hemlock branches and nettles, of the kind Atlin had already learned to use for rubbing his skin after bathing. But there were no corpses of men and small children freshly dead, no skeletons, no skulls; these were the things Atlin had been told whalers kept in the shrines, and the things he had been afraid to find in his father's shrine.

Nit-gass watched silently as Atlin looked about him. At last Atlin asked, almost in a whisper: "Why have we come here?"

"Because it is time," Nit-gass said. "My father Tetacus brought me here when I was a boy like you and made it my own place. Now I make it yours."

"Do we pray to the Four Chiefs here?" asked Atlin.

"If you feel it is good. I pray better on the beaches or by the river or in my canoe. It is as a man feels."

"Are the spirits here? Is the whale spirit in these people?" Atlin pointed to the row of carved figures along the outside wall.

Nit-gass laughed softly. "Some would say so. Those are your ancestors who have been whalers before you. Spirits are where you find them, here, in the woods, on the beaches, on the sea."

Atlin's courage grew with his father's laugh. "May I look at the whale?" he asked.

"Go right up to it. Touch it if you wish."

"Why is its head so big?"

"That is Kot-ske, the sperm whale. You have not seen one like him, but one day you will."

"Is he very strong?"

"Very strong and very brave."

"Will you kill him?"

"Who knows?" said Nit-gass. "But when I see him I shall give him my best harpoon."

Atlin hesitated, looking about him from his new position. "There are no dead men," he said. "No skeletons. They said there would be."

Again Nit-gass laughed, but so loudly this time that Atlin was afraid the spirits would be offended. "Those are not for us," said Nit-gass. "We do not rob graves to make magic so that dead whales will drift to the beaches. The Tsitikat people have a chief, Eskowit, who makes magic that way. We are hunters and our magic is in our harpoons held by live men."

"I have heard the magic of dead men is very strong," said Atlin.

Nit-gass touched his shoulder. "The magic of dead men is in you. It is in me. It is in your grandfather, Tetacus. One day you will understand that. Now we must bathe at the Forks. Take four bundles of the hemlock branches and we will go down there."

Swimming back under the falls seemed easy to Atlin. What he had seen at the shrine, the way his father had spoken and laughed and explained made everything seem at once more real, less frightening—and yet no less difficult. The spirits, it seemed, were farther away than he had supposed. They did not expect such fearful things of a mortal as he had been led to believe. What they did expect was difficult, perhaps very difficult, but Atlin thought he was beginning to understand it.

Back on the gravel beach on the south side of the Kamiss River, Nit-gass arranged his four bundles of hemlock twigs in a line at the edge of the water, told Atlin to do the same and sat down. It was much lighter now, though the mist still hung at the height of the treetops and little wraiths of mist curled along the line of the stream. Nit-gass gave Atlin a head-band of dyed cedar bark, like the one he himself was wearing, and told him to put it on. "I chose this place long ago," he said. "Soon after I had brought home my first whale. Some said that it was not good, that the little swampy pools in the wood are better because they are still, like the sea. What do you think?"

"I think the sea is not still very often."

"Good," said Nit-gass. "You are right. I like this water because it moves and is strong. It is very clean, to wash away the man smell the spirits do not like. It is always cold, and that is good for a man. When he has bathed for many years in cold water, then the cold and the rain and the sea waves do not turn him pale and take away his heart."

"Is it not good to bathe in the sea?" asked Atlin.

"It is always good to bathe in the sea," said Nit-gass. "The sea water is cold, the waves are strong. The sea is the home of the salmon, the seals and the whales. A man who hunts them must know it closely."

"Is it good to bathe in the sacred places, like the Pool of Koptca and the Pool of the Sacred Shark?" Atlin had heard of these places in his grandfather's stories and he knew that war chiefs sometimes bathed in them. But he asked the question now because some of the older boys had said that Nit-gass bathed there.

"For some men," Nit-gass said. "It is good. But not for all. A man should have power before he goes to such places." He

31

stood up. The light was strong now and the mist in the tree tops was turning pink with the rising sun. "It is time," Nit-gass said. "I shall swim in the pool four times and each time I shall dive like a whale, four times. Watch closely the first time. After that you must do the same."

Nit-gass walked a few steps into the foamy edge of the pool, slid into the water and began swimming. He swam very slowly and smoothly through the eddy to the edge of the current, then dived. A moment later Atlin saw him in the eddy on the far side of the pool. He blew water out of his mouth like a whale's breathing, floated a moment, then dived again and swam slowly up the eddy towards the falls. Close under the falls he surfaced again, blowing water forward like the sperm whale's spout instead of straight up like the grey whale's. From there he crossed the current again and came back down the eddy towards Atlin, surfacing for the fourth time directly in front of him. He spouted water and laughed, looking up at his son.

"Are you ready?"

Atlin nodded.

"Then go before me. You need not dive. Just put your head under. But swim slowly and smoothly, as we want the whales to swim. Do not splash or struggle. The current will not hurt you."

The sun had broken from somewhere behind the mountains in the heart of the great island they lived on and the mist in the tree tops was now blood red. Blood red light reflected on the foam of the falls, on the river and on Nit-gass' back and shoulders.

"You have brought the whale's blood," Nit-gass said to his son. "It does not happen often."

Atlin stepped forward into the water that rippled and shone at his feet. He felt the spirits lifting him so that he slipped easily into swimming and was no longer afraid of the cold or the

current. He dived, felt the current press on his body, swam on
and came up in the eddy on the far side. He tried to make the
whale's spout as his father had, swallowed water, sputtered
and almost sank. But Nit-gass' hand was under him. "Do not
try to dive yet," Nit-gass said. "Put your face down only."

Atlin did as he was told the next time and it was easier.
His father was beside him when he raised his head close under
the falls, beside him still as he crossed the current and made his
fourth float in the eddy they had started from. Twice more they
circled the pool together, then Nit-gass said: "You are cold,
Chief. Can you do it once again, alone?"

Atlin felt his chin quivering and clamped his teeth to keep
them from chattering, but he knew he could and pushed
forward towards the current without answer or hesitation.
Nit-gass watched him closely, wading forward in the eddy until
he was chest deep, moving up as Atlin did, meeting him as he
crossed back and following his last float.

"That is well done, Chief," he said as Atlin raised his head
and blew a feeble spout of water for the last time. "You were
cold, but you did not hurry. Now come out of the water with
me."

Somehow Atlin found footing on the rounded rocks and
forced his numb body to make its way to the beach. He could
no longer keep his teeth from chattering, but he was proud
as he had never been before. Nit-gass picked up one of the
bunches of hemlock twigs and handed it to him. Atlin took
it and began to rub himself, but he was still so cold that his
movements were slow and fumbling.

"Rub hard," Nit-gass said, taking one of his own bundles
and rubbing the left side of his chest and body. "Like this.
Make the blood come to your skin. Keep rubbing till all the
leaves are gone."

Atlin's body warmed quickly under the rubbing and in the
growing warmth of the new day. He listened to the rasp of the

hemlock twigs on the father's rock-hard body and wished that he could make the same sound against his own skin.

"Take another bundle," said Nit-gass, as though answering his thought. "Don't be afraid. Rub till the blood comes. It will make you strong so that you will never feel the cold and never grow tired when the whale has taken your harpoon."

"Should we not pray?" asked Atlin. "Mother tells me to pray when I bathe."

"There is time enough for that," said Nit-gass. "Tomorrow I will teach you a whaler's prayer to the Four Chiefs."

Altogether Atlin went to the Forks with his father four times, on four successive mornings. On the fourth day Nit-gass told his crew they were ready and that evening Atlin went out for the first time in the whaling canoe.

4. The Start

As soon as Nit-gass gave the word he was ready, his crew and that of his younger brother Kon-gass went to work to prepare the canoes and the gear. It was a busy and exciting time that Atlin always enjoyed, but now he was a part of it. He stood beside his father, watching far more closely than he ever had before, a little disturbed to be apart from the other small boys who ran about and shouted and sometimes got in the way, quite silent because his thoughts were so busy. Without seeming to pay much attention, Nit-gass noticed everything that was done, joking and laughing with his men, occasionally giving an order or suggesting something to Tokwit.

Both whaling canoes were drawn up on cross-logs in front of Nit-gass' house. The crews rubbed their black hulls to a glossy polish with cedar bark mats and bundles of rushes, then greased them with deer fat so that they would glide smoothly and silently through the water. As a finishing touch, Tokwit and the other steersman took a freshly cut spruce bough in each hand and gently brushed the full length of the hulls along both sides to give them a fresh scent that would not be offensive to the whales.

As soon as his canoe was ready, Nit-gass told the men to carry it down the beach. He watched them as they set it down

35

carefully on log rollers at the water's edge, then turned to Atlin. He was smiling and his eyes were very bright.

"This is the time, Chief," he said. "This is when your heart gets ready. You'll know it one day. But you've got to watch everything, make sure everything's right. When you're over the whale's back, it's too late."

Atlin understood what he meant. Men were passing back and forth, carrying the whaling gear down to the canoe—lines and line-baskets sealskin floats, food and water boxes, paddles, the long killing lance, the chisel-bladed cutting lance. It was a confusion of many things that he had often watched before, but a confusion that would lead in the end to the orderly arrangement of everything that belonged in the big canoe for the whale hunt. His father was telling him that all this did not come about by accident, that things could be forgotten or misplaced in the canoe unless somebody watched, and the man who had to watch was the whaler himself.

"Tokwit is a careful man," Nit-gass said. "And wiser than I am. But that is not enough. The whale chief must know for himself; now, when the canoe is still on the beach and again when he stands up to strike the whale."

Again Atlin thought he understood, but he said: "Tokwit was a whale chief, before his leg was caught in the rope and the whale twisted it. Why is it not enough that he should watch?"

"Because it is for the whale chief himself and no one else. The whale is his and he must be ready for it. Ask Tokwit. He will tell you so."

They were walking up the beach again, towards the house. Atlin asked: "When I am a whale chief, can Hinak be my steersman, like my uncle Tokwit?"

"Hinak is a slave," said Nit-gass. "Slaves do not go with the whaling canoes."

"You have told him he must go everywhere with me," said Atlin. "He plays with me and sleeps beside me and hunts with me. He is my brother."

"Does Hinak want this, to hunt whales with you?"

"He is my brother," Atlin said again.

"Whatever a man wants very much comes to him. You are still young. When the time comes you will know if he should go with you."

As they came into the house Atlin's mother, Aneetsa, met them. Like Nit-gass, she wore a band of cedar bark around her hair and in it a sprig of green hemlock. "You are ready, Hawil?" she asked.

"Yes, Hakoom," Nit-gass answered her. "It is almost time to go."

"You will take him too?" She touched Atlin gently as they walked through the centre of the great house.

"Yes."

"You are sure he is ready?"

Nit-gass was lifting down one of his great yew wood harpoon shafts. "You know he has been to the Forks with me. My father Tetacus has said it is time for him to go with the canoes. What he sees now he will take into himself. It will grow in him and be part of him."

"He is still so small," said Aneetsa. "You will not hunt Kot-ske when he is with you?"

Instead of answering, Nit-gass turned and held out the heavy harpoon shaft to Atlin. "Take it, Chief. Hold it up in your hands and carry it to the canoe for me. It is my best shaft."

Without thinking, Atlin put up his hands, palms outward, and received the shaft across his chest, in the same grip as his father had held it. The unexpected weight made him shift his feet and his small hands only just held the thickness of the polished wood, but he felt a thrill of excitement at his father's trust and smiled confidently when he realised he was holding the full weight.

"You see?" said Nit-gass. "He knows already how a harpooner must hold his shaft. Take it with you, Azma, take good care of it. I will bring the spare shaft."

Atlin swung the great shaft on to his shoulder and started out with it. Behind him Nit-gass took down his second shaft. Aneetsa picked up the whaler's box, which held the harpoon points in their protecting cedar bark sheaths, Nit-gass' special whaling charms and the other small things he took with him for repairs or emergencies. It was always her special duty to carry this down to the canoe and she held it now carefully cradled in her arms.

"Nit-gass," she said. "Please be careful of him."

"He is my son. He carries my heart with him."

"You can hope too much for him, too soon. He has not yet found his tumanos, his guardian spirit, and the whale spirit will not guard him as it does you."

"Am I not strong enough for both?" asked Nit-gass. "Have I not brought many whales safely to the beach?"

"All that is true," she said. "With ordinary whales like Ma-ak and the Sorefaces. But do not hunt Kot-ske when he is with you."

Nit-gass smiled. "I shall not hunt Kot-ske. But if he spouts close to the canoe—who knows? Perhaps the young chief would have brought him to me to look for my harpoon."

"I do not want it when you are both together," Aneetsa said. "It is enough to lose one man."

Nit-gass frowned. "You have said too much. It is not good the whale chief's wife should think against him. Now bring the box and we will go down to the canoe."

At the canoe, Nit-gass set the spare harpoon shaft across the thwarts on the left side, with the killing lance and the chisel-bladed cutting lance. While two of the paddlers were lashing

these weapons to the thwarts, he took the other shaft from Atlin and set it at rest in the groove between the two "ears" of the canoe's high prow. Aneetsa put her precious box in Nit-gass' place, just ahead of the forward thwart, and at once began a slow whale dance, circling the canoe in the direction of the sun.

Tokwit handed Atlin the harpoon head with its bone barbs and lanyard of whale sinew. "Give it to Hawil, your father," he said.

Nit-gass took the head, uncoiled the lanyard, then reached over and set the head firmly on the point of the shaft, forcing the carefully tapered wood into the grooved socket between the barbs. Aneetsa continued her dance, her hands swimming on edge before her, the thumbs raised like the dorsal fins of killer whales. She was still in her twenties, a light and graceful dancer, but she made her movements slow and rolling and heavy, so that she seemed like a whale swimming lazily over a smooth sea. As she danced she sang softly of good weather, of a whale swimming towards shore with her husband's harpoon and of the welcome the village would prepare for it, changing her song with each circuit of the canoe.

Nit-gass paid no attention to her, but turned to his whaler's box and took from it one of the sharpened mussel shells that made the cutting blade of the harpoon head. He slid this very carefully into the cleft between the barbs, pressing it firmly into the heavy coating of spruce gum that protected the lashings holding the barbs to the lanyard. Then he tied the lanyard against the shaft with two or three light threads of yellow cedar bark. Aneetsa completed her fourth circuit of the canoe and turned towards her husband, raising her hands, palms outward, in the sign of honour. A moment later she began walking up the beach towards the great house, still very slowly and with the rolling movements of the whale.

Nit-gass looked carefully over the canoe, the coils of line

between each pair of thwarts, the four inflated sealskin floats, the spare floats beside Tokwit's place in the stern. He saw the food and water boxes, the line baskets, the paddles, then glanced up the beach towards Aneetsa. "Hakoom has gone to rest," he told Tokwit. "It is time to go."

"Hatslatsatl," Tokwit said sharply to the crew. "Come on."

The men picked up the canoe and carried it into the surf. Nit-gass swung Atlin aboard and climbed in himself. Two successive waves curled and broke against the high prow, sending the spray flying, then they were riding swiftly over the smooth easy swells towards the setting sun. Atlin drew in a deep breath of excitement and looked about him.

He was squatting comfortably on the left side of the canoe, just ahead of the forward thwart. His father was in front of him, paddling steadily. Behind, in the space between the two forward thwarts, were the first and second paddlers, with one of the inflated floats and a coil of heavy cedar bark rope set on top of the line basket. In the space behind them were two more paddlers, another float and a longer coil of lighter line; behind these were still two more paddlers, this time with two inflated floats and a coil of still lighter rope on top of the one on the right. Finally Tokwit sat in the stern, with the food and water boxes and a pile of deflated floats in front of him, ready to be blown up when a whale was struck.

The men sang as they paddled, often interrupting themselves to talk and joke as the canoe rode on into the shining, golden path of the western sun. From his place in the stern Tokwit asked: "How far this time, Chief?"

Nit-gass kept his paddle moving evenly. "It has been calm for many days," he said. "The Sorefaces will be far out. When daylight comes we should see the Crystal Mountain beyond the Long Point in the north."

"That is very far," said Hagilt, the first paddler. "If the

whale should die out there we would tow more than two days to bring him back to the village."

"When the Soreface feels my harpoon," said Nit-gass. "He will swim gladly towards the village. He will be proud to be the first of the year to come there."

The second paddler, a very dark broad-faced man who was sitting directly behind Atlin, was the crew's joker. "Ho," he said, "and will he tow the canoe all the way or must we paddle a little?"

"That depends on many things," said Nit-gass solemnly. "Have you made good prayers lately?"

The crew laughed because they knew that Shiyus, the second paddler, was not a serious man. But Shiyus, as usual, had the last word. "The best I know, Chief. But they were not loud enough for Kot-ske, the sperm whale, to hear them."

The men laughed again, for they all knew something of Nit-gass' ambitions, but it was a laugh of confident and contented men and Atlin felt suddenly the strength of his father's power, which held them all together. They began to sing again, one song following upon another, the paddler keeping time to the rhythms, the slender blades bending to each stroke of the tireless arms. Nit-gass handed Atlin a spare paddle and he too paddled and sang as the sun went down and the stars came out over the summer sea. They held on through the soft night with its gentle breezes until about two hours before dawn, when Nit-gass signalled they had come far enough. The high graceful prows of the canoes swung towards the south and two paddlers in each canoe held gently against the northwestward set of the current. Atlin was tired, but still excited. Nit-gass held out a corner of his bearskin robe.

"Get some sleep, Chief," he said. "Before the sun is over the mountains we shall be hunting."

5. *The Hunt*

WHEN ATLIN woke he was stiff and cold and it was still dark. Then he realised his father's movement had wakened him. Nit-gass was crouching, one hand gripping the gunwale of the canoe. "Listen," he said.

Almost at once Atlin heard a series of explosive hisses, like the blowing of porpoises but louder and starting more sharply. He peered into the misty darkness, but could see nothing. The sound was repeated, seeming closer, then there was a mighty slap on the water, followed by the heavy crash of a great body falling back.

Everyone was awake now. From the stern, Tokwit said: "You knew the place well, Chief. Shall we follow them?"

"No," said Nit-gass. "They are restless. They travel too fast and we should lose them in the darkness. There will be more."

"The stars are gone," said Hagilt. "The weather will change."

"It is nothing," Nit-gass told him. "A little fog that will go with the sun."

Atlin could hear seabirds moving and beginning to call. The dawn was not far off. He felt the tenseness of his father's body relax, but knew he was still listening. He was cold and felt disappointed because there had been no chase of the whales.

"What if there are no more, Hawil?" he asked.

"Don't worry, Chief," said Nit-gass. "There will be. It is a good place here by the Long Rips. The tides come together and there is much food. You must remember that when you are a whale chief."

Very slowly the first daylight came creeping through the mist. They could see the prow of the canoe and the harpoon shaft slanting against the pale water. It was the time Nit-gass loved best of all, the time of promise, the time of life's stirring to the beginning of the sun's return, when anything might happen and the whole day lay ahead, unspoiled as yet by any flaw or failure.

"It will be a good day," he told Atlin softly. "We shall see the backs of many whales. In one of them my harpoon will find its place."

The light spread around them, diffused through the fog. The ocean heaved in long smooth swells, grey but with dull white lights where the currents twisted the surface. Beyond sight in the fog Atlin could hear the slap and rustle of wavelets stirred by the Long Rips, the splash of feeding fish, the splatter and stir of scoters and murrelets and cormorants. Nit-gass stood up in his place and stretched, looking back over the thirty foot length of the canoe to see that all was in order. Tokwit was already soaking some of the deflated floats so that they would be ready if a whale was struck. The others were all in place, the line coils on top of them and leading out over the starboard side of the canoe. He reached over and handed the loop of the harpoon lanyard to Hagilt, who quickly secured it to the ten fathom coil of one-and-a-half inch line in front of him.

"We shall find whales today," said Nit-gass. "But they are passing through. You will have to break your paddles to come up with them."

The Hunt

"Unless one has eaten too much and is lazy, like Wewiks," said Shiyus.

Everyone laughed because Wewiks, the fourth paddler who was also the man who blew up the spare floats and sat just behind Shiyus, was very fat.

"If we only had thin men like you to blow up the floats," said Wewiks, "all the whales would get away."

"That is true," agreed Tokwit. "If the fat whales work as hard as Wewiks they will be hard enough to catch. But perhaps Gakatas, the little bird will be sleeping when we find one. Where shall we hunt, Chief?"

The answer came at once, a succession of sharp, explosive sounds from whales blowing in the fog immediately ahead of them, towards the rips. The canoe was already starting through the water as Nit-gass dropped to his knees and picked up his paddle. Atlin paddled with the others, his heart pounding with excitement. The sound came again and Nit-gass shouted for speed as he glimpsed a dark, humped back through the fog and saw it draw slowly down under the water; but he already knew in his heart the canoe could not catch them. The chase held on, encouraged as the whales surfaced once again; then they sounded and were lost in the fog.

As the men rested and the canoe drifted on the tide, Nit-gass turned to Atlin. "Did you see them, Chief? They wouldn't wait for us."

"I saw one," said Atlin, "but he was not very close."

Nit-gass laughed. "We will take you closer to the next one, Chief. So close you will smell his breath and see the little crabs crawling on his back."

"Hawil," said Atlin, "what is Gakatas?"

"He is the little black seabird that looks out for the whales. It was the tumanos, the special spirit, of your great-grandfather. The whales were always quiet for him and he killed many."

As Nit-gass spoke, the first whisper of the north-west wind came down through the fog. The water rippled, slopping against the canoe. Within moments the fog had rolled away from them, inshore and towards the south. The sunlit ocean was wide about them and over the fog-bank, the tallest of the mountain peaks sparkled white and clear against blue sky. Nit-gass' quick eyes saw his brother's canoe about a mile away. He signalled it and was answered. Then the sperm whale broke water to seaward. Every man in the canoe saw it, but no one moved.

Nit-gass drove his paddle and shouted a single word of command—the steersman's word: "Hatslatsatl," which means "Come on." The men obeyed and the canoe started through the water like a frightened fish.

From behind him Atlin heard Tokwit shout a warning: "Take care, Hawil."

For answer, he saw his father raise his left arm and swing it to show the line on which he hoped to intercept the whale, then drive his paddle deeply and strongly again. Paddling steadily himself, Atlin watched the whale. It was alone, travelling steadily at the surface, now drawing down until it almost disappeared from sight, now raising its great, square head to blow its forward slanting spout. Because he was so large it seemed to Atlin that he was travelling very slowly. But Nit-gass knew that the canoe's best speed would barely intercept him and he called again: "Come on" in a voice of thunder. The whale surfaced and blew again, and they were within a hundred yards of it. They were no longer intercepting its path. The great body had turned almost squarely out towards the open sea.

Nit-gass shouted again, drove his paddle in three more furious strokes as the whale's body drew down, then sprang to his feet and seized his harpoon shaft. A moment later he was securely balanced with his right foot firmly on the double

46

thwart behind him, his left on the starboard gunwale of the canoe. From there he could see the water disturbed by the great tail flukes and the bubbles of the whale's submerged passage. The canoe was too far to the right and Nit-gass signalled Tokwit again. Seconds passed as the canoe raced on, became a minute, almost two minutes.

Then the whale surfaced again, still fifty yards ahead, still off the port instead of the starboard bow. Tokwit changed direction slightly and they began to gain on him. Atlin saw Nit-gass flex his knees, heft the heavy harpoon shaft, settle his feet still more firmly. The whale's enormous tail flukes were lazily sweeping the water not twenty feet ahead of the canoe's prow and Nit-gass shouted once more to his men for the burst of speed that would place him where he could strike. Then the whale's head drew down again and this time the huge grey back humped up behind it. Tokwit, watching the canoe's prow draw almost level with the tail flukes, swung out a little. It was well that he did so. A moment later they flung high in the air, throwing a sheet of water over the canoe. Atlin gasped and choked under the shock and weight of the deluge. The canoe's bow wrenched over violently in the surge and Nit-gass dropped down from his stand to avoid being flung overboard. A moment later he leapt up again, the water-laden canoe rolling under him, and peered ahead for signs of the whale's passage under water. But he knew, and Tokwit knew, that the great whale had sounded into the depths and they would not see him again that day.

6. *The Kill*

STILL SHOCKED and startled by the immense violence that had come from the seemingly slow and lazy roll of the whale, Atlin could only sit where he was and remember the enormous tail, towering above them in the bright sunlight and hurling streams of green water in every direction. Then he realised that his father, far from being concerned or disappointed, was happy. Still perched precariously on thwart and gunwale, Nit-gass half turned and looked down at his son. "We were close to him that time, eh, Chief? How do you like it?"

His father's normal, half-joking tone and easy words were complete reassurance for Atlin, but he still spoke with awe in his voice: "His tail was bigger than the canoe."

Nit-gass turned completely around and laughed heartily, looking back at his startled crew and the disordered canoe. It was half full of water, wallowing awkwardly in the gentle swells, the gear bobbing and floating about between the thwarts. The fifth and sixth paddlers were automatically bailing water overboard. Hagilt was staring up at where he had last seen the tail flukes against the sky. Shiyus and the fourth paddler behind him were still backing water with their paddles as though to swing the canoe still farther away from threatening destruction. Only Tokwit in the stern was completely calm.

"Your tumanos is not with you today, Chief," he said. "The whales are restless."

Shiyus stopped his aimless paddling. "Perhaps the Chief's tumanos is working for all of us," he said. "If he had struck Kot-ske—ay-ee, we should all be swimming now."

Nit-gass laughed again. "Kot-ske would have swum for us, and farther than we wanted. He was turned the wrong way."

"But you would have struck him if you could," said Hagilt reprovingly. "Could we have killed him or would he have killed us?"

Nit-gass shrugged his shoulders. "Who knows? With a good thrust I should have found his heart. He would not be so strong then."

"It is a bad day," said Tokwit gloomily. "Everything is restless and moving. Nothing stops to float or feed."

"We have the Young Chief with us," said Hagilt. "Perhaps the whales do not know that yet."

"Kot-ske has started him well," said Shiyus. "He threw enough water on him to wash him in the sea."

"True," said Nit-gass, "but the Young Chief was laughing when the rest of you still sat with your mouths open." He let his jaw drop and his body droop and his eyes roll skyward until everyone roared with laughter. Then he straightened up, waved his powerful arms and rocked the waterlogged canoe violently with his feet. "Now let us get rid of Kot-ske's water and put the gear in order. It's time we showed the Young Chief we are men enough to catch even the restless whales."

He turned away at once to examine his harpoon and shaft and lanyard. Behind him the alderwood bailing scoops went steadily to work, scooping the water against the side of the canoe and throwing it out in easy rhythm. Soon the canoe floated light and dry again, the floats were restored to their

49

places, the lines re-coiled and ready. Kon-gass had come up with the second canoe and they set off together to hunt again, working southward along the edge of the rips.

It was, as Tokwit said, a flighty day. The north-westerly breeze freshened, little fleecy clouds fled across the sky, birds scattered and wheeled over the dancing water, occasionally a fish jumped without pattern or purpose. And the whales were still restless. Twice more travelling schools were sighted and twice the canoes gave chase but could not come up with them. Atlin's muscles ached from paddling, the salt spray dried on his face and lips and his legs were cramped. But he thought of these things only at intervals. He wanted to see his father strike a whale. He wanted the day to be successful, so that his claim to a place in the canoe could not be questioned. He wanted to see what these men had seen and feel what they had felt when whales were struck and the heavy lines raced out over the side and the sealskin floats bobbed on the water.

Soon after noon, Nit-gass turned back towards the shore. He was well beyond the usual hunting grounds and now that he had made his try for the sperm whale he was no longer anxious to strike his quarry so far from the village. The north-westerly had freshened again with the afternoon sun, breaking whitecaps against the steady tidal current, but the canoes rode easily across it and soon the dark-green, forested hills of the land came in sight under the high peaks of the mountains.

"The little bird is with us all today, Chief," said Shiyus.

"How is that?" Nit-gass asked him.

"If you had killed that great Kot-ske we should have been towing him tonight and tomorrow night and two nights after, so he must be with us. And if he had not been with Kot-ske your harpoon would have found a home."

Nit-gass laughed. He always enjoyed the second paddler's moods and theories. "The little bird could have done otherwise and brought honour to everyone—dancing and eagle-down for

Kot-ske's saddle, a new name for the Young Chief and a winter's feasting for all of us."

The sun was well down towards the horizon and the breeze of the afternoon had faded by the time they could distinguish the entrance to Kashutl Inlet and the long point in front of the village. The day was almost over and Atlin felt a keen sense of disappointment; in a little while he would be at home on the village beach and everything would be as it had always been. Perhaps his father and the crew would not want him in the canoe again because the whales had been restless and hard to approach.

The whitecaps had flattened to little soft wavelets and red and black lights ran on the water when he saw Nit-gass straighten in front of him. Almost at the same moment he saw the whale blow half-way across the entrance to Kashutl Inlet. It was a broad vertical spout and Nit-gass knew the whale at once for a humpback. He watched it disappear, show again, spout again. He was sure then that it was a solitary bull, travelling lazily, less than two miles offshore. Behind him his tired crew had seen nothing. Only Tokwit had noticed the straightening of his chief's shoulders and the intent set of his head.

"What is it you see, Hawil?" he asked.

Atlin answered before his father could speak. "A whale," he said, "in the inlet."

Nit-gass turned to him in astonishment. "You saw him? Before you were born I named you 'His eyes see far off.' It has become a true thing. The young chief is right," he told Tokwit and pointed to where the whale spouted a third time. "Look."

"You think we can meet him?" Tokwit asked quietly.

"We can meet him in front of the village beach," Nit-gass answered. "Put me beside him and I will strike him to the heart."

Tokwit gave his command and the paddlers, fully aroused

now, laid to their paddles as though they were fresh from a full night's sleep. Nit-gass stood up and looked back over the gear. He told the third paddler to straighten his coil on top of the line basket, told the fifth paddler to clear the third float so that it would pass freely out over the fourth. Atlin paddled steadily with the others; excitement was high in him again and the day's meaning was restored to him. As he watched his father's easy movements and heard his calm words he felt himself a part of the hunt, bound to the others in the achievement that would be theirs when the whale was struck. Nit-gass glanced down at him. "When I strike," he said, "keep well down, keep still, keep close against your side of the canoe. Do not paddle."

Nit-gass turned back to look for the whale. There was a risk that it might go down and bury its head in one of the kelp patches off the village point; if so, they could not hope to find it before darkness came. But he saw at once that the whale was still travelling on in his line, sinking briefly under the surface, rising to blow, drawing lazily down again.

"He is an old one," said Tokwit. "He will fight."

"Only put me close to him," answered Nit-gass. "I will strike deep enough to calm him."

They were closing fast now, the whale still unaware of them. He was past the point, squarely in front of the village, when Tokwit swung the canoe to bring it up from directly behind him. The whale surfaced again, turned on his side and showed one of his bulky fifteen-foot flippers above the water. Nit-gass picked up his harpoon and took his stance again on the forward thwart and starboard gunwale. Atlin watched as he flexed his legs and settled his balance, then swung the great shaft to limber his arms and shoulders. After that he stood with the shaft at rest across his chest, the palms of his hands turned outwards as they gripped it, elbows bent at his sides, his eyes on the whale. The whale drew down again directly in front of the bow and Tokwit said sharply to his crew: "Come on."

Nit-gass, following the whale's underwater passage, signalled Tokwit to swing the canoe out a little, to the left.

"When he shows again, Hawil, we shall be with him," Tokwit said quietly.

The paddles bent and bit hard. A rustle of water fled against the canoe's sharp prow. Nit-gass watched the whale and signalled with the harpoon point, so that Tokwit would keep the canoe close, yet not so close that there would be danger from the swing of the tail flukes when he surfaced again. The sun was near setting and the water was oily still except for the gentle run of the swells, ground-swell and lighter cross-swell from the afternoon's wind. In spite of the watery whisper of the canoe's passing, the paddlers' dip and thrust and the occasional straining grunt of one of the men behind him, Atlin thought he had never felt a deeper silence than this swift and deadly approach.

Suddenly a broad ripple sped against the cross-swell, picking up the bright light of the western sky on its folds. A moment later the water heaved and the whale blew, a sharp, explosive snort like the crack of a mighty timber, and the spout curved high above them, raining down in fine spray. For the first time Atlin smelt the whale's breath, powerful and pungent. The paddlers drew up, past the swinging tail flukes, along the great, curved body until Nit-gass could see the flipper almost under the prow. All the while Tokwit eased in, closer and closer, until canoe and whale were racing silently side by side not more than three or four feet apart. The mottled grey back of the whale showed red gold in the setting sun. The same light gleamed from Nit-gass' body and the haft of his spear, and for a moment Atlin felt that both man and whale were creatures from the supernatural world.

The whale's head drew down and his humped body sank

slowly with it. Nit-gass swung his harpoon so that the head pointed down and the butt of the shaft was high above his head. In the stern, Tokwit watched the tail flukes as they swung over, closer and closer to the canoe. When they were so close that he could have touched them with his hand and he knew that the outward swing must start, he said sharply:

"Strike." In the same instant Hagilt reached forward and touched the calf of Nit-gass' right leg with the tip of his paddle.

Nit-gass struck, with all the power of his body and all the confidence of his heart. He felt the blade bite through skin and blubber and drive deep, down and down into the great thick body below him. As the blow spent itself he freed his shaft with a quick turn of the wrists, breaking the yellow cedar threads that held the lanyard to it in the same movement.

The Kill

The lanyard drew violently into the water and the coils of heavy line began to leap away from in front of Hagilt. Nit-gass dropped instantly down into the bow space, the harpoon shaft still in his hands, his eyes on the disappearing line. He did not crouch down, as harpooners usually did after the thrust to be out of danger from the lines, but set his shaft back in its resting place, glanced at Atlin and laughed aloud. "Now he has it, my good harpoon," he said. "Now you will see, Chief, how the whale can swim."

From the moment of the thrust the crew had worked to force back the canoe away from the whale. Hagilt threw over the first float and already the coil of line by the third paddler was leaping out. As the third float went overboard the whale spouted and Nit-gass, watching closely, saw a deeper redness in the red-gold spray. A moment later the thick-barrelled body broke water awkwardly, falling on its side, swivelling round towards the open sea. Nit-gass turned quickly and reached for the killing lance, which the fourth paddler had ready for him.

"Throw the fourth float over," he said sharply.

The whale broke again. He was no longer heading out to sea, but directly towards the canoe, right on the surface. "Hold the bow to him," Nit-gass called urgently and stood ready with the lance. The whale came on, towing lines and floats in a great circle behind him. Thirty feet short of the canoe he dived, humping his back and rearing his tail flukes high.

Nit-gass and Tokwit shouted together: "Tlitsa, tlitsa. Back away. Hard."

The paddlers responded and the canoe slid back away from the whale's path. Several seconds passed and Atlin crouched behind his father, his eyes wide and fearful. Somewhere under the water, close by, was the whale; how or from where he might burst out upon them Atlin did not know, but he knew they were in danger. Nit-gass glanced about him, watching the water warily, his lance at the ready in the hope of turning a sudden rush or break. Then the whale's great tail reared up and smashed down on the water, exactly where the canoe had been at the moment of his dive. They were well clear of its force and fury, but water rained down on them and into the canoe. The bailers went to work at once.

"Go forward," Nit-gass ordered. "To the left." He meant to bring the canoe to seaward of the whale and behind him. The tail smashed down again, with the same fury and in the same place, four more times in quick succession. Then it disappeared.

"He has not found us," Nit-gass told his crew. "He is deeply struck. Watch on the sides, paddlers. Watch astern, Tokwit my friend."

He himself watched over the bow, tensed and ready. At the village the people had seen the fight and were swarming down the beaches from the houses. Several canoes had put off. Time passed and all was quiet. The sun had gone now, but the western sky was still red and gold. Then Nit-gass saw the fourth float moving on the water, drawing away from them. He signalled Tokwit to start the canoe after it. The whale showed, well inside them and headed directly for the beach less than a mile away. There was blood in his spout and his movements were slow.

"Come on," Nit-gass shouted and was echoed by Tokwit in the stern. The other canoe, which had turned in before the attack, was now much closer to the whale's track.

Nit-gass called across the water to his brother: "Strike him for me, Chief Kon-gass, and I will give you his tongue and one of the flippers."

It was a Chief's traditional gesture rather than a call of need, for Nit-gass knew the whale was tiring fast and his own canoe could soon come up with it again. The other canoe went in on the whale, but did not close well so that Kon-gass'

stroke, from too far out and too far back, made only a light wound.

"He is too quick," said Tokwit. "He should wait."

"No," said Hagilt, "Waiting would not help. They have no heart for going close to the whale."

"It has helped," said Nit-gass simply. "He is still swimming towards the village."

The whale had stirred from the thrust in a driving surface flurry that carried him much closer to the village beach, where the people were dancing and calling to him and singing songs of welcome. Tokwit, urged his crew in pursuit and they were already close when the whale slowed his rush and turned north-ward about a quarter of a mile offshore, as though disturbed by the sound and the waiting people. Nit-gass had mounted a second harpoon head on his shaft and the fourth paddler had two more floats ready. But Nit-gass looked hard at the whale, then set the harpoon down in the groove at the prow and picked up the lance again.

He looked back at Atlin. "I am going to kill him for you, Chief," he said quietly. "Stand close to me."

Atlin stood up beside his father and saw the whale only a little way ahead of them, high in the water, his great tail still thrusting powerfully, but slowly. "Is he dying?" Atlin said.

Nit-gass nodded. "Yes, but he still has the strength to go far." He turned back towards Tokwit. "It is time," he said. "The water is shallow here and he will not dive again."

Tokwit brought the canoe up easily along the left side of the whale, watching the slow swing of the tail flukes. He knew that all the strength had not gone out of him and that Nit-gass hoped to kill at once, before the last of the light was gone.

Atlin watched the whale's back as they drew closer and closer to it. It seemed almost black now, though still reflecting red lights from the sunset sky. He could see the lanyard trailing from the great wound of his father's first thrust, just behind and above the huge flipper. He could smell the whale again, he could see the lumps on the whale's head that gave him the name "soreface", the little crabs that crawled in hollows on his back, the sucking creatures that clung to him. His throat was dry and tight with excitement and his chest hurt from trying to breathe quietly. Then he heard Nit-gass talking quietly to the whale. "Whale," he said, in the words of the whaler's prayer. "Whale, I have your heart in my hands now. I have given you what you wanted, my good harpoon. My son, the young Whale Chief is watching you. Do not turn outwards. Keep close to the shore. Take this lance and carry it to the beach of my people who are waiting to welcome you."

With the lance balanced in his hands, he stepped up to his place on the gunwale and the forward thwart. Tokwit watched the flukes, holding the canoe at a steady distance to be ready for the death flurry. Then he gave the signal. Nit-gass struck twice, deeply but very swiftly, just forward of his harpoon lanyard. Atlin watched the long, whalebone point of the lance drive in, withdraw, drive in again, then the paddlers wrenched the canoe away from the whale's fury and he dropped to his knees as Nit-gass jumped down beside him.

In his agony, the whale rolled on his side. One of his long flippers came high out of the water and he thrust violently with his tail flukes, hurling sheets of water over the canoe. He submerged briefly, came up in a violence that lifted his thick body half out of the water, fell back and drove wildly for the beach. He stranded himself in the shallows and spouted thick blood that dyed the dark water around him. Then a long, heaving swell, larger than the others, lifted his body and swung it forward on its right side so that the creases on the under side of throat and belly showed plainly.

Tokwit swung the canoe to bring it in to a stern first landing in the breakers beside the dead whale. "He brought you home, Hawil," he said solemnly. "It does not happen often. Honour him greatly, for he has honoured you and the Young Chief."

7. *The Seal Hunt*

THROUGH THE rest of that summer Atlin went out only occasionally in the whaling canoe. Nit-gass did not take him when the weather was uncertain or when he expected to be out for several days or when he intended to hunt the sperm whale because Aneetsa, his wife, had persuaded him that it was not yet time for the boy to be exposed to such risks.

"Even as it is," she had said, "you are taking him with you two or three years before most whale chiefs take their sons."

"It is good for him to learn when he is young," said Nit-gass.

"There is plenty of time for learning. He will not be strong enough to drive the harpoon for at least four more years."

"He can learn best when he is young. He takes the whale's movements and the sea's movements into him with his eyes and ears and hands and makes them part of him."

"It is enough to do that when the weather is good and when you do not go too far out."

"He learns quickly," said Nit-gass. "He grows stronger every day. He will become a great whale chief."

"The more reason to keep him safe," she said. "You might not find another son like him. Take him with you to your shrine and your bathing. Teach him a whaler's ways so that he will find his tumanos and be safe—if a whaler is ever safe."

60

Nit-gass' father, Tetacus, told him much the same thing, but in different words: "The whale canoe is not a place for a young boy. It is good that he should go with you sometimes, but not often. First he must learn to go without food and sleep and his body must become strong against wet and cold."

"For his years," said Nit-gass. "He is very strong."

Tetacus was sitting on his special seat in front of the long house, looking out over the village beach and the ocean beyond. His brown, leathery face, criss-crossed with deep lines, was serious. "You and I know how cold it can be when the rain and the storms come and we must be out there many days. We are strong men, but it reaches to our hearts and makes us weak. Such things are not for a young boy. The cold may shrivel his heart so that it never grows again."

"Is it not best to learn when you are young? Do we not say that small children take the wise words of older people into them with the food they eat?"

"There are other things to learn," said Tetacus. "And other ways of learning. He must become a true chief so that men will like him and follow him. Teach him to hunt seals and sea lions and sea otters, so that his eyes become quick and his arms strong. From that he will also learn the ways of the sea."

"It is true," said Nit-gass. "A boy must learn many things slowly if he is to become a man. But I want the whale spirit to be strong in him."

"Then let it grow slowly, as it grew in you and me and our fathers for many generations. Let him learn to go hungry and without sleep for many days together. Let him bathe often when the water is cold. The whale chief's tumanos does not come to a man when his belly is full or his body is warm and rested."

As soon as the whaling season was over, Nit-gass began to spend time with Atlin. It was already autumn weather, often foggy, sometimes raining, with stormy winds from the south-west that made the surf pound along the village beach and break in great white plumes against the rocky islets of the point. Many of the people had gone to the Hotsath River in Kashutl Inlet to catch and smoke the spring salmon and dog salmon there were running in to spawn. Nit-gass went there for a few days to see that all was going as it should, then he and Atlin came back to the main village. "That is not work for Chiefs," he said. "You and I will hunt seals."

Atlin had seen the weirs that trapped the dog salmon, and the huge spring salmon lying on the shallows where the spear-men could easily reach them. He had thought the busy camp an exciting place to be. "Why did we go there, then?" he asked.

"Because a Chief must be with his people. It is not necessary all the time, but he must know that everything is done well—with the seals and halibut and herring as well as the salmon, because these things belong to him. When the Chief is careless, his people become careless."

Atlin understood this readily enough. He knew that the fishing streams and the beaches where the herring spawned and all the hunting places and the ocean in front of the tribe's territory, as far out as the horizon and beyond, belonged to the Chief. Certain men had the right to set the traps or do the hunting or the fishing, but the Chief had to tell them when it was time to start and they had to bring him certain shares of everything they caught or killed. Later, the Chief would give these back to the people in the winter dances and potlaches. He had learned all his life that there were many things a chief had to do and a number of things he was not allowed to do. Once he had lost his temper in a game with Witamis, the war chief's son, who was larger and stronger and older, and had begun to fight with him. Tetacus, his grandfather, watching from his seat by the long house, had come down at once and separated them. He took Atlin to one side and told him: "A chief must never quarrel. It will make him less in the eyes of his people. If someone tries to quarrel with you, turn your back and walk away. Do not answer."

Remembering this, Atlin said to his father: "It is hard to be a chief."

Nit-gass laughed. "You cannot always do as you want. No man can. But you will not find it too hard. You will grow into it, learning a little all the time."

They had come back to the village to go sealing and Atlin was eager to go. But Nit-gass made him bathe first, night and morning on four successive days. During that time Atlin ate only a little dried salmon and drank occasional sips of water from a special bowl through a hollow bone, using it like a straw. They bathed from rocky ledges on the little islands off the village point, because, Nit-gass told him, these were the sort of places seals liked. It was exciting there on the misty mornings and at night when the waxing moon showed from behind the clouds. Often it was raining and the surf boomed behind them on the windward side of the islets. Even on the leeward side it leapt at them and pounded them until Atlin's body was sore and stiff and bruised as well as very cold. Towards the end of the time his head felt light and his body seemed a free thing of its own that he could no longer control or direct, though it felt clean and strained inside and out. Yet somehow he repeated the prayers Nit-gass had taught him and floated and swam holding his head high out of the water like a seal that is undisturbed. When he told his father how he felt, Nit-gass said he had done well. "Some time, when you feel like this, you will know the whale spirit has come to you."

They went sealing early on the morning of the fifth day. It was calm and foggy but the surf was still breaking heavily from the wind of the previous afternoon. With Hagilt, they launched Nit-gass' light, knife-prowed sealing canoe under the lee of the village point and rode out through the curving waves to the longer and smoother swells beyond. Hagilt paddled in the stern and Nit-gass told Atlin to take the bow paddle while he checked the harpoons.

Nit-gass' sealing harpoons were hemlock poles, about ten feet long, with two pieces of yew wood carefully set in at the head to form a Y. The two spear heads were much like small whaling heads, with horn barbs that formed sockets to fit on the yew wood foreshafts and a long bone point with a series of small barbs worked along one side. A light lanyard of sinew was bound into each head, coming back from the foreshafts to a single lanyard that extended along the main shaft.

Nit-gass set his harpoon heads firmly in place on the fore-shafts, then secured the lanyard lightly along the main shaft with tyings of yellow cedar bark. He showed the points to Atlin. "Hagilt made these," he said. "Most of the hunters use mussel shell, as we do for the whales."

"These are good," said Hagilt. "They don't break. A hunter can use one many times. But it is better to use mussel shells for sea lions so that the barbs go deep."

"The sea lions are strong," Nit-gass told Atlin, "and too heavy to pull with the canoe. I do not hunt them unless the people are hungry and there are no seals."

Hagilt laughed. "You do not like to eat them so well as seals. Nor do I. Where are we going, Chief?"

"To the rocks off Round Hill Point," said Nit-gass.

Round Hill Point was at the north end of the village beach, about three miles from the village itself. Atlin had been there several times, walking along the beach with Hinak to scramble over the rock ledges of the point, tease the starfish and anenomes in the tidal pools and hunt for crabs and small fish. He could not see the point now because of the grey wall of fog that enclosed them, but soon Nit-gass told him they were close to it. He fastened the harpoon lanyard to a sixty-feet coil of light cedar rope, then fastened the end of the rope to the forward thwart.

"When I strike the seal," he told Atlin, "you must look after the coil. Make sure the line goes out smoothly. Hold it with your hands when it comes near the end so that the canoe will be following the seal. Then there will be no sudden jerk when the pull comes against the thwart."

As he spoke, Nit-gass balanced the shaft of the harpoon on the palm of his left hand, the points angled slightly upward, his right hand on the finger grip that was set into the butt. He was watching the heaving grey water ahead of the canoe, but without strain, his body relaxed and rolling with the movement of the canoe in the swells.

"There," he said and pointed the harpoon to the left of the canoe's prow.

"I see him," said Hagilt. "He's down."

Nit-gass turned to Atlin. "Gently, Chief," he said. "Keep your paddle soft. Don't let it scrape on the canoe or rustle in the water. Under water the seal hears everything."

They paddled easily for some fifty yards, then Nit-gass said quietly: "Enough."

Atlin held his breath and watched the heaving water. It had begun to rain through the fog and big drops spattered the surface. The seal's black head came up suddenly, on the breast of a swell, turned away from the canoe. Nit-gass launched his harpoon almost in the instant of its appearance and the shaft flew in a low arc, the points striking the water just behind the seal's neck. There was a flurry and a splash as they seal dived and the coiled line began to leap from the canoe. Atlin tried to grab the line, missed, then caught it. For a moment he held too hard and was almost pulled out of the canoe. But he let it slip through his hands, gradually increasing the pressure as the seal's run slowed. "Good," said Nit-gass. "Feel him. Do not give it to him too easily."

The light, narrow canoe was moving swiftly through the water now and Atlin eased out the last two or three coils to let the pull come on the thwart. The seal surfaced briefly and dived again. "He swims hard," said Nit-gass. "He will tire quickly. Take in line when you can." He had recovered the harpoon shaft from the water during the seal's first run and was fitting new heads and a new lanyard to it.

The seal thrashed on the surface and dived again, but Atlin felt him weakening and began to recover line. Soon the seal was alongside the canoe, dark head and sleek body gleaming in the grey light. Nit-gass handed Atlin a heavy club from the bottom of the canoe. "Kill him quickly, Chief," he said. "Good. Now roll him into the canoe." He put his weight on the side of the canoe so that the gunwale was almost level with the water and Atlin half slid, half rolled the thick round body into the canoe. Nit-gass handed him a knife and he cut out the two heads, both of which were firmly set, beyond the barbs.

"He didn't pull very hard, that one," said Hagilt. "He wanted to come with you."

Nit-gass handed Atlin the harpoon. "You've seen how we do it, Chief," he said. "Now get one for yourself. We should have ten in the canoe before the fog lifts."

8. The Shaman's Dance

THE WINTER that followed was the richest and most exciting the Hotsath people had ever known. There was blubber and whale oil, berries and herring spawn, seal meat and salmon meat for everyone, and plenty to spare. Expecting this, Nit-gass had "thrown" his sacred crystal early in the year—that is, he had taken the crystal from the box where it normally lay with his other hereditary possessions and had pretended to throw it, first to the north and then to the south, announcing to his people that he intended to invite the Tsitikat people and the Kashutl people to a great winter dance and potlatch. The news of this intention had travelled swiftly to the Tsitkats and Kashutls as canoes visited up and down the coast during the summer and the people were ready when Tokwit came with several canoes to deliver the formal invitation for his Chief.

The heavy rains began towards the end of October and soon the salmon streams were flooding, washing out the weirs and hiding the shallows so that the salmon could no longer be caught and were left to their spawning. Most of the people moved back to the main village and the fires burned brightly in the great cedar houses while the November gales roared and the rolling waves battered the beaches and points. Everyone was preparing for the feasts, practising songs and dances and playlets, polishing bowls and feast dishes, counting up salmon fillets and whale blubber and boxes of oil. It was two years since Nit-gass had given a great winter dance and the wealth of the tribe had built up steadily through that time.

Atlin's training went on. Nit-gass sent him to bathe in the freshwater pools morning and night through the waxing of the moon, warning to him to eat and drink as little as possible and to sleep sparingly. "It is good to do so now, when it is easy," he said. "Later you will fast longer, go without sleep for many days and nights together, swim without feeling cold that would make other men numb and helpless."

Atlin was glad of these duties that took him out on his own when it was too wet and stormy to go to the hunting and fishing grounds. Sometimes he took Hinak with him and Hinak was quick to notice his increasing strength and endurance. "Chief," he would say, "when you are a man you will be able to hold your breath longer than a whale." Or "Chief, when you swam here a week ago your hands shook so much you could hardly rub your body when you came out. Now they are strong and calm as though you had slept by a fire."

Tetacus undertook to teach him the songs and dances he had to learn for the feasts. For this Atlin had less patience. "Why must I learn to put every word in the right place? Why must my foot go this way and not that way?"

"Because it is so," Tetacus would explain patiently. "Because that is how the songs and dances have come to us, from our grandfathers and great-grandfathers who learned them first from the spirits and brought them back to us. If you do not know them properly the people will laugh at you and say you are not a great chief."

"Is it not enough for a chief to kill whales and guide the hunting and fishing?"

"No," said Tetacus, "it is not enough. A chief must be all things to his people. Without them, he is nothing, his possessions are nothing. Watch your father. No man has brought in more whales. But he always has time for his people. He speaks kindly to everyone. When he walks through the village he recognises the children and knows their parents. What the people do for him he gives back in feasts and dances. So the people follow him and honour him."

As the old man had intended, Atlin felt a little ashamed of himself. But he said: "It is hard to remember the words exactly."

"They have been remembered exactly by many before you," said Tetacus. "You must make them yours so that all the people can see that you have a right to the privileges your father will give you at the feasts."

So Atlin learned and was ready when the guests arrived from the neighbouring tribes and the feasts and dances began. The great winter dance, or the Shaman's Dance as it was called, was always the same. It lasted for nearly three weeks and was a time of great confusion, practical jokes, clowning, acting, dancing, singing and speech-making. Yet a certain order ruled everything about it and many serious purposes were served—gifts were given and debts were paid, rights and privileges were claimed and recognised, new names were given to many people and sacred possessions were displayed.

Atlin knew the general order of the Shaman's Dance almost by instinct—it had been a part of his life, as it was for every member of the tribe, from earliest childhood. Twice before he had been captured by the "wolves" in the early stages of the dance, to be carried off into the woods for several days and brought back to receive a new name. He had been too young then to take full part and the words and dances that went with the names were sung and performed for him by older people. But this time he would have to bear his own part.

After the ceremonial arrival of the guests, the Dance began, as usual, with several days of gradually building excitement.

Wolf calls sounded around the houses, now very close, now far away. People drummed on hollow planks and sang songs and shouted to keep the mysterious wolves away. There were rappings on the walls of the houses during the nights and strange men, painted and feathered, ran through the murky red light of the fires, upsetting things, stealing blankets from the sleepers and creating confusion. Everyone pretended to be very frightened and upset and there was much talk of guarding the children from the wolves. But one by one the children who were to be named and initiated into the secret society of the Dance were stolen away. Atlin, who was one of the older ones, was the last.

This part was all familiar to him. The "wolves" were men of the tribe wearing wolf skins and with their faces painted black. Hagilt and Shiyus were two of the wolf leaders. There was night travel along trails into the deep woods, brush shelters among the tall trees and great fires whose light glimmered on tree trunks and hanging moss, making the woods themselves into a huge house with the boles of cedars and hemlocks for walls and the dim recesses of their high tops for a roof. Hagilt and Shiyus kept up their pretence of being supernatural beings, but they rehearsed his songs and dances and made sure he was perfect in them.

One night, when the "wolves" had drawn back with their captives into the deep woods, Hagilt said: "Remember, Chief, this is no ordinary time. Your father is giving you a great name: 'He-brings-live-whales-to-the-beach.' It came to him from his grandfather's grandfather."

"He told me this," said Atlin. "It is because the soreface whale swam to the beach when I was with you in the canoe."

Hagilt went on as though he had not heard: "In the feasting he will seat you in the high chief's place, between Eskowit of the Tsitikats and Nukumas of the Kashutls."

Atlin remembered a visit of the previous winter to the

Tsitikat village. "I do not like Chief Eskowit," he said. "He is a loud man. He does not like my father."

Hagilt spoke urgently. "You must not show you think such things, Chief. Chief Eskowit is your guest. But he is jealous of your father because the Hawil brings in many more whales with his harpoon than Eskowit can with his magic."

"Has he magic?"

"So they say. It is witchcraft. He calls to dead whales at sea through the mouths of corpses propped up on the beaches, to make them drift in to his territory."

"I know," said Atlin, "and he has skulls in his shrine and bathes with a corpse on his back. It is powerful magic."

Shiyus moved closer to them from the shadows. "Perhaps," he said, "but the Tsitikat people have only had two whales while your father has brought in ten. I think your father's tumanos is better."

"That may be," said Hagilt, "but Eskowit is a powerful chief and he is a guest. You must be kind to him and treat him well or you will disgrace us all."

"I do not like him," said Atlin, "but I shall honour him and treat him well."

9. *The Spearing*

FOR A DAY or two more this first great stage of the winter dance went on, the wolves creeping out to the edge of the woods near the village, the people drumming and singing, making complicated and ridiculous plans to trap the wolves and save the children. Sometimes the drumming and singing of the village was timid and pleading, sometimes it was loud and fierce and demanding. Sometimes the wolves were snarling and ferociously active, sometimes they were mild and friendly. But gradually the village sounds became bolder and stronger and steadily the wolves became tamer and milder. But the mock skirmishes between the wolves and the people were as violent and funny as ever. Atlin watched from the edge of the woods with the other captives and laughed with delight at the antics of the people they ran from a mock attack by the wolves, falling over each other, rushing into the water, upsetting canoes, screaming and yelling with excitement and pleasure. The thing that really marked the time apart was that everyone—even the most dignified and elderly people of the village—took part in the pretence and the horseplay. He saw his father deliberately upset three canoes in quick succession, his grandfather running and pretending to fall down, Tokwit limping away and shaking his fist at the wolves, even his quiet mother running and laughing with all the others.

The Spearing

In the very last stages, while the wolves hovered, whistling and calling with their captives at the edge of the woods, the people began a great drumming, led by a prancing man on the roof of the long house. Using hardwood sticks they beat out a series of thundering rolls on the hollow planks. When they stopped the man on the roof scolded them: "How do you think that will bring the children home? They could hardly hear it if they were at the edge of the woods."

The people scolded back at him. "Give us another leader," they said. "It will never be any good with you up there."

But they drummed again when he told them, much louder than before and keeping better time. Atlin thought he had never heard such fierce and powerful sound—it was like the surf of a great storm or thunder in the high mountains.

"You were better that time," the man on the roof shouted down to them. "You started slides in the mountains and floods in the rivers and rolled back the tide on the beach. But you must do better still. You must make the stars fall and the trees tremble and the whales dance and fly like eagles. Then perhaps the wolves will hear you."

So they drummed again and yet again, and after the fourth time Hagilt and Shiyus told the captives to shout for their parents. The younger ones, frightened by the noise of the drumming and the strangeness of everything about them, played their parts in earnest and set up a tremendous screaming and wailing; even Atlin, who had been named twice before at Shaman's dances of other years, found himself shouting his loudest. Parents came running from everywhere, quickly gathering them up and carrying them or dragging them to the shelter of the long house.

So the great festival went on, half in earnest because the people believed that the spirits were never far away and knew that rituals and taboos and privileges must all be properly observed, yet never far from the fun and gaiety of songs and laughter and practical jokes.

The captives recovered from the wolves were kept secluded from the main festivities for four days after their return, hidden behind a huge cedar bark curtain stretched across the full width of the long house. Atlin remembered this part vividly from the other times, the blaze of the great fire in the centre of the long house that shone redly on the smoke-blackened planks of the roof and flickered in points of light through the curtain, the passing of dancers' shadows, sounds of singing and speech-making, laughter and solemn talk. Once each night he and the other novices, danced in a long procession through all the houses of the village, still wearing the kilts and capes of fir twigs that the wolves had given them in place of their usual clothing. But on the fourth night these were taken from them and gathered into a great bundle to be burned at the end of the winter dance in a ceremony that would free the village completely from the power of the wolves.

On the fourth night the novices behind their curtain could sense a subtle change in the great house. It was, they could feel, crowded with people. The fire burned more brightly than ever before. There was less confusion, less practical joking, more order and yet somehow a greater excitement than ever before. Suddenly three or four men began singing together, then suddenly a great chorus of voices crashed in upon them. Four times, with a pause between each, this fierce and demanding chorus was repeated. It crashed into silence and there was a pause that seemed to Atlin as loud as sound itself. The silence was broken by a single great cry of several hundred voices and with that the full length of the curtain dropped to the floor. The novices sat with bowed heads before the crowded long house.

Raising his head only a little, Atlin looked up and saw his father standing by the leaping fire, dressed in his chief's robe of sea otter skins. Tokwit stood near him with two men in long grey wolf masks. Another man came forward, pretended to swallow a great draught of whale oil, then spat a gushing jet at the fire that caused the flames to leap higher and brighter than ever. Nit-gass swung his arm in a great commanding gesture that quieted all the waiting people. Then Tokwit spoke in his mighty speaker's voice: "Listen, all you people, for the ones who have come back from the woods will sing their songs for us."

One of the masked men came back to the novices, took Atlin by the hand and led him forward to stand beside Nit-gass. Atlin raised his head and looked boldly about him at the people massed along the sides of the long house. He knew it was a special time for him and though he felt uneasy with all those eyes upon him, he knew he was ready for it. He felt his father's hand on his shoulder, saw Tokwit step forward to speak again. Then, very abruptly, a man in a chief's blanket and a chief's head-dress strode forward into the open circle before the fire. Atlin saw that it was Eskowit, the principal chief of the Tsitikats.

Tokwit drew back and looked questioningly at Nit-gass, who nodded his head slowly. Tokwit stepped forward again and spoke: "Chief Nit-gass is honoured that his brother of the Tsitikats should wish to speak at this time. He is sure that what is to be spoken must be of very great importance."

The great crowd had murmured uneasily when Eskowit stepped forward. The murmur swelled to an angry protest at Tokwit's words. Visiting chiefs had no part in the Shaman's Dance except as guests; later, in the feasts that followed, they would take their rightful places and speak as they wished. But the rites of the Dance were for the people of the tribe and no one else. Tokwit raised his voice, commanding silence: "The Chief of the Tsitikats will speak," he said.

Eskowit stepped forward again and faced the crowded long

house. He was a man in his late twenties, tall and big, with thick black eyebrows on a jutting forehead that shaded narrow black eyes. His mouth was almost delicate, with a thin moustache above it but a heavy jaw below. He began speaking at once, in a high, harsh voice that carried clearly through the building. He praised Nit-gass, praised the Hotsath people, praised the splendour of the Shaman's Dance. Yet he gave to all his words and phrases a faintly contemptuous ring, as though he were an adult praising a performance of children. Atlin felt his dislike growing with every word and reminded himself of Hagilt's warning. Beside him, Nit-gass was calm and unmoving, but Tokwit glanced questioningly back at his chief from time to time.

Eskowit turned directly towards Nit-gass. "You have shown us many wonderful things, Chief," he said. "And displayed many great possessions. We are glad you have invited us. Yet in all you have shown us we have missed something." At this point he turned away so that his voice reached straight out to the crowd again. Atlin felt his father's hand stir slightly on his shoulder. Eskowit's mocking voice had a sugary softness. "We have seen no spearings. Can it be that the Hotsath people have grown timid?" He threw back his blanket and showed the heavy scarring of his upper arms. "Or can it be that no man among you has a spearing privilege?" He turned again towards Nit-gass. "I ask these things, Chief, because I am sure there has been a mistake. You would not wish to forget the traditions of your ancestors."

There was a moment of shocked silence, then a roar of protest. Smiling, Eskowit went back to his seat. Cumalik, the principal Hotsath war chief, leapt to his feet and half-a-dozen lesser chiefs with him. Even Atlin knew that Eskowit's words, in that place and at such a time, were a deliberate insult. Nit-gass stepped forward, his hand raised for silence, and Atlin saw he was smiling—not a forced smile, but the smile Atlin had seen on his face when the canoe drew close to the whale. His voice was slow and soft and unconcerned.

"The Tsitikat chief has spoken many words, but in the end, he has said only a very little thing. For many years now we have kept our spearings for the whales at sea, as the Chief well knows. He has no need to do so, since he brings the whales to his beaches not by harpoons, but with magic."

The crowd laughed and Eskowit glowered. But Atlin could feel that the mood of the people was still strained and uneasy; he saw that Cumalik had gathered the other war chiefs about him and that all, instead of sitting, were crouched as though ready to spring, their hands on their war clubs. Nit-gass went on to talk of the ceremonial spearings the Hotsath people had used at Shamans' Dances in the past. "The arms and sides of the Chiefs were pierced by the spearmen, but they were strong men and showed no fear. It was not a great thing in our winter dances, as it seems to be with those of the Tsitikat Chief, but we gave it some value." Nit-gass paused and looked across at Tetacus. "I would have the Chief, my Father Tetacus, tell you now of the changes that were made."

Very slowly Tetacus came forward into the open space by the fire. His body was still straight and strong and he was taller than Nit-gass by fully as much as Nit-gass was taller than Atlin, so that the three of them made a range of steps that pleased the people and made them laugh affectionately. The Shaman's Dance, in which every detail was normally planned in advance, was suddenly playing by itself, and they were quick to notice that the details, as well as the players, still gave it full dramatic effect. Tetacus spoke deliberately and with great dignity. "My son, the Hereditary Chief of the Hotsath people, has spoken truly. We have uses other than play for our spears. It is true that we used the spearings in our winter dances. Many years ago, before I became old and made my son your Chief, the spearing was done to Callicum, the father of Cumalik, in both arms. Callicum was the war chief, stronger and bigger than any man here today. When the spears were thrust into both his arms he laughed aloud and for four days and four nights he would let no one cut them out." The old man paused, leaning on his staff and looking about him at the people. "When the spears were cut out," he went on. "The wound in the left arm did not heal. Callicum's arm and shoulder became as hot and red as the heart of that fire and his flesh swelled to bursting. Then the spirits entered into him so that he screamed and raved until he died. He was the strongest man of all our people, yet he died." Again Tetacus paused and looked about him. There was not a sound in the great house except the dropping of logs in the fire and the rush of the winter wind on the walls and over the roof. "After that I went into the woods for many days," Tetacus told them. "I learned that the spirits were angry because we had made a game of the spearings. So I ordered an end to them and there have been no more spearings in our winter dances since that time. Those who hold the privileges have not displayed them."

Atlin saw a troubled frown crease his grandfather's forehead. "It is a little thing," the old man said. "But it is not a little thing that a guest of the Hotsath people should be displeased with our Dance. So I have remembered an ancient privilege of the Hotsath whaling chiefs that has not been displayed in my lifetime or my father's." Tetacus turned and spoke briefly to Tokwit, who went away and came back almost at once with Hagilt and Shiyus. Atlin saw that each of the three men carried two sealing harpoons, set on short shafts. Tokwit handed his at once to Tetacus, who held them before him for all the people to see.

Atlin felt his heart pounding and his throat dry and moved slightly, as though to run to his grandfather. At once his father's hand was on his shoulder, restraining him. "It is nothing," Nit-gass said softly. "Watch and do not be afraid."

The Spearing

Tetacus dropped his staff and let the sea-otter robe fall from his shoulders. "This privilege," he said, "with its story, I have already passed to my son, Nit-gass. It is no longer mine to name. Now I wish him to display it to please our guest. Because I cannot name it I will give him a sign by which he can know it."

Tetacus handed one of his spears to Tokwit. Then he gripped a pinch of skin on the outside of his left thigh in the fingers of his left hand and, in a single swift movement, thrust the other spear through it. Without pausing, he passed the shaft to Tokwit, took the second spear from him and thrust it into his right thigh. The watching people uttered a great sigh, then began to talk. The old man silenced them: "I have given you the sign, Hawil," he told Nit-gass. "Let our guest see that we do not slight him." He folded his arms then and stood waiting.

Nit-gass stepped forward and began at once to speak: "The spearing of which my father, the Chief, has spoken, came to us from the olden times. It is called the Spearing of the Legs."

Atlin listened with a feeling between fear and pride as his father told the ancient story in all its large ceremonial details. From time to time he glanced at the blood that ran slowly, unheeded, from the spear points thrust into his grandfather's thighs. Nit-gass' story was new to him. It told of one of his ancestors, a great whaling chief, who had brought his canoe in upon two whales, a large one and a smaller one, swimming side by side. Instead of closing properly with one of the whales, he had picked up a second harpoon, and holding one in each hand, had thrust at both whales at the same time. Since he was a man of great strength, both harpoons had gone home.

As any whale chief knew, to strike a second whale before the first had been brought to the beach and properly honoured was an offence against the whale spirit and it would have been natural enough if the harpoons had torn loose and both whales had escaped. But the strength of the Chief and the power of his thrusts was such that the whales could not break loose, though they fought mightily and towed the canoes where they chose for four nights and four days.

As Nit-gass told the story, a group of men came in and began a dance that matched his words. Two, a large man and a small one, were the whales; another was the chief with his two harpoons; the rest paddled an invisible canoe so skilfully that the canoe itself seemed to be there in the firelight. Standing close to Atlin, Tokwit whispered: "In the end, they will spear you and your father. It will hurt very little. Stand straight and keep your face calm, then fold your arms as Tetacus did. In that way you will make Eskowit look foolish and his insult will be wiped out."

The Whale People

Raised in the ways of his people, Atlin accepted the warning without surprise, though his heart beat faster and he wondered how much hurting was "very little." He listened to his father again, determined to follow his words and be ready at the climax. Tokwit made him move forward so that he stood level with Nit-gass, on his right and about six feet from him. A moment later the dancers passed between them, the whales towing the invisible canoe, the whalers holding a line in each hand and trying to check them, the paddlers breaking water.

On the fourth day of the great struggle, Nit-gass told the people, the Thunderbird looked down from his high mountain and decided it had gone on long enough. With a roar of wings he swooped down, seized the tail flukes of the whales in his talons, the canoe in his beak and dragged them—the weight was so great he could not fly properly—to the village beach. There he left them, all except the Whale Chief and the Whale Chief's son, whom he carried away with him. Many days later, the two returned safely to the village, but the marks of a harpoon thrust showed plainly on the right leg of the Whale Chief and the left leg of his son. Ever after that, they had great power over whales. No matter where the harpoon entered, it held firmly and often whales died outright from thrusts that seemed in no way mortal.

As Nit-gass finished his story he set his legs apart, planting his feet firmly, and raised his arms in front of him until they were level with his shoulders. Watching him closly, Atlin did the same. He heard the dance coming up behind them, saw the whales pass through and circle away to either side. Then he felt strong fingers grasp the skin of his left thigh and, a moment later, a burning pain as the spear went through. His leg trembled and his eyes clouded for an instant so that the light of the fire leapt in strange shapes. But through it all he held his head high and watched Nit-gass. Calmly and deliberately, Nit-gass folded his arms and Atlin followed his movements.

The Spearing

"We have shown you a spearing, my people," said Nit-gass in a very loud voice. "You can see for yourselves it is a small thing. Now let us go on with the Shaman's Dance."

But the people began to laugh and shout and drum on the hollow planks. Then the drumming leaders stood up and gave them the time and they drummed until the walls shook and their arms were sore.

10. Hotsath Winter

THOUGH the Shaman's Dance went on for several days more and was followed by a great potlatch, the spearing remained the high point for Atlin. The wound healed quickly after the barbed point was cut out later in the ceremony, but it left a heavy, ridged scar on his brown thigh which pleased him greatly. Nit-gass, Tetacus, Tokwit, Hagilt and many others praised him for the part he had taken. Nit-gass added a word of warning: "It would have been better if it had not happened. Eskowit will be our enemy now."

"He did not like us before," said Atlin.

"True," said Nit-gass. "But he is a man of evil temper. He would be great and is not. His heart is twisted in him."

"Can he hurt us?" asked Atlin. "Hagilt says he must have great magic to make the dead whales drift in to the Tsitikat beaches."

Nit-gass laughed. "He also has currents that set in well for he Tsitikat beaches. Often we have to paddle hard against them to tow in our own whales. When you hunt seals or sea lions anywhere beyond Shark Island you will find the drift sets that way very fast. No, I am not afraid of his magic."

Atlin, who had not yet learned the power of ocean currents, did not fully understand. "Do you think the whales would come there without magic?"

84

Nit-gass shrugged. "Who knows? Dead whales drift some-times to our own beaches and we make no magic for them."

"Yet there is magic," said Atlin, still puzzled. "You have great magic yourself. Everyone says so. When the whales feel your harpoon they swim slowly and go towards shore instead of out into the ocean."

"The magic is not mine. It belongs to the whale spirit who helps me. If it were mine it would work for me all the time. Yet sometimes the whales are wild and I cannot come up to strike them. Sometimes they break away after the harpoon is in them. Sometimes they swim far out into the ocean and will not die. Sometimes they turn and break my canoe. You know these things have happened, because I have told you the stories."

"How do you know when the spirit is with you?"

Nit-gass considered the question carefully. He had just finished whipping a new lanyard to a sealing harpoon and was turning it over and over in his hands. "You feel it," he said at last. "It is in your heart, in your arms and in your legs. Your men can feel it when they are behind you in the canoe. When all that is so, you will go in very fast and very close on the whale. You will strike at the right moment with all your strength and without fear."

"If you were afraid and did not show it, would the spirit know?"

"Perhaps. But if you do not show it the spirit still helps. Your men cannot know it and your harpoon will still go deeply into the whale. Were you not afraid of the spearing?"

"Not of the spear," said Atlin. "Only of myself. That I might grow weak and faint."

"No one saw it. The spirit helped you and you did not grow weak. But the spirit cannot help a whaler who is not ready." Nit-gass held up the harpoon in his hand, pulling on the lan-yard with the other hand to test it. "Your blade must be sharp and the barbs strong and true. You must know the lines are coiled properly behind you and the floats ready. And when you go in to strike you must not hesitate or draw back too soon. You must send your heart and body with the thrust until it reaches the whale's heart and can go no farther. When all these things are done as they should be, the spirit is helping you. If they are not done well, it may still help you. The whale may swim quietly and towards the beach and may die easily, but it does not happen often."

"Could not a man do all these things without the spirit helping?"

"Yes," said Nit-gass. "But I think the spirit will always help such a man. When you bathe and clean your body, when you go without food and water and sleep for days together, you bring the spirit near you and the things you do will be right. I do not know which is first, what the man does or what the spirit does."

"How will I know when I have found the whale spirit?" asked Atlin, watching the spear as his father laid it aside.

"You will know. Perhaps you will see it. In the olden times men saw spirits more often than today. But we still follow the old ways and the spirits still come, even though they do not always show themselves."

"Have you seen a spirit?"

"I have heard their words when I am alone in the woods or on the beaches. Gakatas, the little bird, has come to me often when I am alone in my canoe. When I took the broken harpoon shaft to the shrine the supernatural squirrel was there, but I did not hear him speak."

"It does not seem very much," said Atlin.

"Other men have seen and heard much more. But it is more important to feel the spirit than to see it. Then your legs will not grow weak when they should be strong and your heart will fill your body so that you feel joy in your arms when you lift the harpoon and laugh aloud when the whale throws water into the canoe. When you feel the spirit you can walk on the back of a live whale with your killing lance and stand like a chief on the village beach to kill him."

The rest of the winter passed happily for Atlin and all the Hotsath people. Even in January, which was called "The-month-of-no-food-getting," there was feasting and plenty for all from the abundant stores of blubber and whale oil, as well as the other foods for which these had been traded with neighbouring tribes. Snow fell and soon after there came a succession of great storms that washed it all away in wind and rain. Stormy weather held on into February, but Atlin bathed regularly with his father through the waxing of each moon and felt himself grow steadily stronger against the cold. He was with his father a great deal now and Nit-gass answered his questions with a patience and solemnity that only occasionally broke into laughter and jokes. "You ask questions like Blue Jay," Nit-gass told him once. "Without looking for the answer that is right in front of you." Then, seeing that Atlin looked glum, he added: "But you are as quick as Mink in learning. One day you will be a wise Chief."

Late in February the storms eased and the canoes went out again. Soon word was brought to Nit-gass that the herring were in Kashutl Inlet and ready to spawn. He went out at once, taking Atlin with him. It was a clear day and they could see the bright flashes of the herring everywhere through the water, but Nit-gass shook his head and told Atlin: "It is not time. This is the false spawning. I have looked at the eggs in the fish they have brought in so far and they are not loose yet. Take the rake now and I will show you."

Atlin picked up the rake, plunged it into the water and brought up half a dozen struggling herring which he shook into the canoe. "Again," said Nit-gass, and Atlin kept on until he had raked thirty or forty. Nit-gass took several in his hand

and slit the bellies with his knife. He showed the eggs to Atlin, still hard and firm and tightly set in the ovaries. "It is too soon," he said. "These will not spawn until the moon is past full."

Tokwit and Hagilt were in another canoe near the shore and Tokwit called over: "There is milky water here, Chief, but it is not much."

Nit-gass steered his own canoe towards shore until Atlin could see the water clouded white from the milt of the male herrings. They were near the line of anchored poles where the people would later set fir branches to catch and collect the herring spawn.

"It is only the false spawning," Nit-gass said.

"Yes," agreed Tokwit, "but you must tell the people to watch closely. It will not be long before it is time to set out the branches."

Nit-gass laughed. "They will watch. It is not enough to be able to fill their bellies with blubber and dried salmon. Every year they look for the herring spawn before it is ready."

"You like it yourself, Chief."

"Not enough to waste the work of putting out the branches for the false spawning. Tell them to fish for the spring salmon that will be following the herring."

"They are doing it," answered Tokwit. "Only this morning Kenim filled his canoe with big fish."

On the way back to the village Atlin asked his father: "Why do the people not know about the false spawning?"

"They do," said Nit-gass. "But it does not happen every year and they forget. If the branches are put out too early they will be no good for the big spawning, when all the water is white for several days together. A chief must know these things or his people will go hungry."

"They are hard to know," said Atlin.

"Only if you are lazy and do not go out to see for yourself.

You can trust someone like Tokwit, but even then it is best to see for yourself."

There was a great spawning of herring that year and by the middle of March the drying racks in front of the village were completely covered with fir branches, each with its load of tiny eggs.

Late in March and through most of April the ducks and geese were passing on their way to the northern nesting grounds. Atlin heard the geese crying and calling when he went to bathe in the early mornings, heard them and saw them through the day, heard them again at night as he lay on his bed in the long house. Everyone was gay and busy and full of life at this time and often, on the darkest nights, canoes went out to hunt the birds that were rafted on the shallow bays over the mud flats. Hagilt was a famous hunter of geese and sometimes Atlin and Hinak went in his canoe. On stormy days they covered the canoe with brush and allowed it to drift in on the rafted ducks from the seaward side, keeping low while Hagilt steered the drift with slight and cautious movements of his paddle. Then, when the ducks were very close, all three shot arrows into them as quickly as they could.

But the night hunting was more exciting. Hinak would set a platform covered with sand across the stern of the canoe and build a small fire on it, which he lighted with a torch brought down from the long house. He took his place in the stern of the canoe, in front of the fire platform, with a cedar bark mat mounted on a light pole. Hinak sat in the bow with a big nettle-fibre net on a square frame. Atlin was in the centre.

They went out on cloudy, moonless nights and hunted the sheltered bays until they heard the whistle and talk of resting and feeding birds, ducks or geese or swans. Then Hagilt put more wood on the fire, took the pole of the cedar mat in his teeth so that it made a dark shadow over the rest of the canoe and paddled gently towards the birds. They were able to come very close so that Atlin and Hinak could see the startled raising of heads on long necks and the confused swimming that always turned from the firelight into the dark shadow cast by the mat in front of the bow. Hinak held the net by its handle, poised over the bow and very still, trying to judge from the sounds how far ahead of the canoe the nervous birds were swimming. When he was satisfied they were clustered tightly in the shadow directly ahead of the canoe, Hagilt would say softly: "Now," and Hinak would launch the net. There would be a great fluttering and squawking, all around them birds flapped and splashed and flew clumsily off into the darkness. But the heavy frame of the net held the trapped ones down and the canoe closed swiftly so that the boys could grab them and wring their necks. Hagilt paddled so stealthily and used the net so skilfully, never allowing the least glimmer of light to fall on the canoe ahead of him, that they were often able to repeat the approach and capture several times in the same bay.

Nit-gass did not go out at all on the duck-hunting that year. After the herring spawning, he started the men to the halibut banks and the sealing grounds, then turned his thoughts to the whaling season. When the weather was stormy he made sure that the men worked on the canoes and the rest of the gear, fretting over the condition of lines and floats, checking his harpoons and lances, even testing the strength of canoe thwarts and the condition of the food and water boxes. In fine weather he and Tokwit, and sometimes Atlin, went out in the sealing canoe to scout for the first coming of the grey whales.

11. *The Sperm Whale*

THE GREY WHALES were late that year and May was an un-
usually stormy month. By the end of it, Nit-gass had managed
to bring only one whale to the village beach. He was not dis-
couraged by this, but seemed more determined and eager for the
hunt than ever.

"Soon the sea will be calm and the whales will be lazy," he
told Atlin one day when they were at the Forks. "It is still very
early."

"We have prayed for the weather to be calm," said Atlin.
"Why do the Four Chiefs not hear us?"

"There are times when no prayers are heard. There have been
summers when the sea was scarcely quiet for two days together and even the sealers and halibut fishermen could not
bring in good catches."

"Would it help to make more powerful prayers? Could we
go to the Pool of the Supernatural Shark?"

"You are young for that," said Nit-gass. "I will take you
before it is time to strike your first whale. But prayers and
spirit-power are not everything. You cannot strike whales
when the canoes are on the beach. When the sea is rough and
the whales are wild you cannot always strike truly and deeply.
In the end it is the whaler's arms and the whaler's heart that

drive the harpoon, even though the spirits help him. You must remember this."

They went out again two or three days later, when several whales were sighted from the beach. Even though it was blowing a fresh westerly Atlin was allowed to go because it seemed that the chase would be a short one. One of the whales had dropped behind and the canoe closed with him rather easily. Nit-gass picked up his harpoon and took his stand on the bow-thwart, but the canoe was pitching so wildly and the wind was so treacherous that Tokwit dared not set as closely alongside as usual. Nit-gass signalled twice, but Tokwit shouted back: "Strike him, Chief, or you will lose him."

So Nit-gass struck, hurling the heavy harpoon rather than thrusting with it. The stroke went into the side of the whale instead of down into his vitals, and he ran from it instantly so that the lines leapt from their coils and Nit-gass ordered the floats over.

Excited and soaked with spray, Atlin watched his father's quick movements as Nit-gass prepared another harpoon. "We must strike him again," he told Atlin, "and quickly. The first harpoon will never hold."

The canoe was travelling swiftly now and the speed seemed to steady it as the high prow brushed the waves aside. Atlin gazed ahead eagerly over the rolling water but could see no sign of the whale. Then he saw the shine of a float on the breast of a wave well out to seaward. He shouted and pointed and Tokwit swung the canoe. But Nit-gass shook his head. "Riding too high," he said. "He's pulled loose."

They came up with the floats and found it was so. "Haul in," said Nit-gass. "Coil the lines carefully. It is a day for whales. Put me closer next time, Tokwit."

"Not unless we come up under his lee," said Tokwit. "The waves will break the canoe on his back."

"Let it break," said Nit-gass and Atlin saw the white gleam

92

of his teeth as he shook the spray from his hair and face. "This time tie the light line on to the end and the small float. We'll make him tow us home."

"To his home or ours?" asked Shiyus mildly. "His is too deep for me."

Nit-gass roared with laughter. "If he took home a gloomy one like you the whale people would chase him out again."

"It is the Chief's day," said Hagilt. "Put him close, Tokwit, and the people will come down to carry us up the beach."

"It is for the Chief to be bold," said Tokwit. "And for the steersman to be wise. This is no day for swimming."

It was Shiyus who saw the whale, well to seaward of them, visible for a moment on the face of a swell, then lost as his high, narrow spout shattered in the wind.

"Kawod," said Nit-gass softly. "The sei whale." He had just fitted a new shell blade to his first harpoon and secured the lanyard to the shaft. Atlin watched as he shaded his eyes and gazed after the whale. The expression on his face was disbelief, changing to a fierce joy. "Come on," he shouted. "He's lazy and he's across the wind."

The paddlers started the canoe and Tokwit said: "He is longer than ten spans. He will drown us."

"He is across the wind," Nit-gass said again. "Take me close in the lee of him and I will give my harpoon to his heart."

The whale had dived. When he broke water again they were less than a hundred feet from him, behind and to the left. The canoe rode easily, quartering the waves towards the long, low curve of his blue-black body. Atlin plainly saw the little dorsal fin, set far back, felt the partial easing of the waves as they came into his lee. "Gently," said Nit-gass. "He is lazy. Don't frighten him."

"Tell him not to frighten me," said Shiyus, "when you give him that little salmon spear of yours."

For once Nit-gass did not laugh. Atlin knew he was saying

the whaler's prayer and tried to find the words himself. They were very close now and Tokwit had to look behind him to judge the swing of the tail flukes. The whale drew down in the water. Tokwit signalled. Nit-gass struck, freed his shaft and leapt down. For a moment, it seemed that the whale had felt nothing. His body drew down until only the little dorsal fin was showing above the surface. Then a great surge boiled up on the waves from the thrust of his flukes and the coils of heavy line began to leap over the side, guided by Hagilt's paddle.

Only the first float was out when the whale surfaced again and blew. There was blood in his spout. "He has it in his heart," Nit-gass shouted. "I have killed him."

The whale dived again, almost at once, and ran, taking the last three floats. Then he surfaced and slowed. Nit-gass reached over and grabbed the light line out of the water. Hagilt dropped his paddle and held on too. The canoe began to pick up speed.

"Take hold, Chief," said Nit-gass. "In front of me. Feel him. It will do you good."

Atlin stood up, took hold of the taut, wet line and felt its throb. The whale began to move faster. The canoe shuddered as it drove against the waves. Hagilt took a wrap on the bow thwart and shouted to Nit-gass and Atlin to ease the line down and let the thwart take the strain. The rope cracked against thwart and gunwale and the canoe flew through the water, whipping a sheet of spray from every wave top until Atlin could hear the hiss of the bow wave over all the other sounds. The men were singing and in the stern Tokwit watched and steered. Nit-gass laughed a great laugh of joy and exhilaration. "Kawod is fast and strong," he told Atlin. "Ma-ak and the Sorefaces will never give you a ride like this. Enjoy it while you can, Chief. It will not last."

As though to prove him right, the whale's strong surface rush began to slow. The line slackened, jerked taut, slackened again. The floats bobbed and danced on the waves and ahead

94

of them the whale rolled heavily. Nit-gass and Hagilt began to recover line. "Let it go," said Nit-gass and dropped the line. He turned to Tokwit. "Take me in. I will kill him here before he takes us farther."

"He has swung away from the wind," said Tokwit. "We cannot go as close as we did before."

"As close as you can," said Nit-gass and picked up the

killing lance. He took his stand on the thwart and gunwale and Atlin saw he was holding the lance in one hand, balanced at his side. The whale was travelling very slowly now, tail flukes sweeping wearily from side to side in a narrow arc, his body heaved and rolling on the following swells. The canoe drew close, pitching and sliding, now threatening to crash against the whale's bulk, now falling off to a distance of ten or fifteen feet. Nothing was still or steady even for a moment and Atlin wondered how anyone could hope to make a killing thrust. Then the canoe lifted on a swell and, through a moment of terror, seemed to hover over the whale's back. In that moment Nit-gass jumped and the ready paddles backed and swung the canoe clear of danger. Atlin saw his father slip once, recover his balance and run forward along the whale's back as far as the little flipper that showed when he rolled. There Nit-gass made two swift and fearful thrusts. The whale shuddered, drove with his tail and forced his body half out of the water. Nit-gass drove his lance into the blubber, dropped to his knees and held on. The whale spouted feebly, with a flat, despairing whistle, then rolled and pitched Nit-gass into the heaving sea. He swam a few strokes clear of the whale and the canoe was alongside him. Atlin and Hagilt helped him climb aboard, still holding his bloody lance. His chest was heaving and he coughed and spat out salt water, but his eyes were bright as he handed Atlin the lance and turned to look at the whale. It was quite dead, rolled on its side, white throat and belly gleaming in the sunlight, the little flipper lifted in what seemed a gesture of surrender. "Whale," said Nit-gass. "You have been very good to us to die so quickly and not to break our canoe. We could not expect such a great one as you to go quietly to the village beach. No whale like you has been brought to our village since my father's father's time, but my people will know how to honour you when we bring you there. It was because my son, the Young Chief is with me that you did not break the canoe. I am glad he has felt your strength and seen your dying. Now float high for us and make the sea calm and the wind quiet, so that we may take you quickly to where my people are waiting to welcome you."

"I told you it was the Chief's day," said Hagilt. "When did you ever hear him make a better prayer?"

Even Tokwit laughed at that, though Atlin was shocked that

Hagilt should joke at such a time. Nit-gass said: "Even Shiyus must have made some good prayers to bring us a whale like this one. When the people see him they will carry us all up the beach."

They towed the sei whale through the whole of that night and brought him to the village beach in the mid-afternoon of the next day. The people met them, wading into the swells, picked up the canoe and carried it on their shoulders to its resting place just below the long house. There Tetacus met them in his chief's robe and greeted Nit-gass as he stepped from the canoe. "The whale people have done you great honour, Hawil," he said. "For this you will be remembered always."

About a month after this, Nit-gass went whaling and did not come back. Atlin had been left behind and was sitting with Tetacus in front of the long house when he saw the canoe coming. At first it was only a distant speck, then they could see it was coming very fast; then Tetacus stood up and shaded his eyes. Standing beside him, Atlin strained to see his father in the bow and could not. Instead, the harpoon shaft stood straight up, lashed to the bow thwart. People were beginning to come out of the houses.

Tetacus sighed deeply and set his hand on Atlin's shoulder. "You know the meaning, Chief?" he asked.

"Yes," said Atlin. "My father is dead." He felt as though a great weight was pressing on every part of his body, from his feet to his head. Tears stung his eyes and were bitter in his throat, but he did not cry.

"You are really the Chief now," said Tetacus. "You must go down to meet them, alone. When Tokwit turns the canoe to beach it, you must ask: where is the Hotsath Whale Chief? Then the people will know you are Chief. Go now."

Atlin walked slowly down the beach, watching the canoe's approach. He could not feel what had happened and the tears no longer burned in his eyes. He was remembering what Tetacus had told him.

He stood at the edge of the water, waiting. When Tokwit turned the canoe and started to ease it in, he asked: "Where is the Hotsath Whale Chief?"

"He has gone to the village of the Whale people, Hawil." Tokwit stepped wearily from the canoe and the paddlers stepped out behind him. Atlin saw that the lines and the floats were missing.

"It was Kot-ske, the sperm whale, that took him into the sea." Tokwit said. "We searched a long while, but we could not find him, so we came to tell you."

12. *The Dream*

THE DAYS immediately after the death of Nit-gass, while the people mourned, were a time of numbed confusion for Atlin. At first he did not really believe his father was dead and wondered how long he would have to stay "in the village of the whale people". Aneetsa, his mother, tried to tell him through her grief that there was no return from this place. But in the general mourning of the people there was no such certainty; Nit-gass had been so great a man, so clearly out of the ordinary, and the memory of his presence was so vivid that many believed he actually would return. Even Tokwit would not altogether commit himself, but it was his description of what had happened that allowed Atlin to understand for himself.

"The Chief found the sperm whale," he said "As he had meant to find him for many years. He was lazy and at ease, rolling on a calm sea, his head as high out of the water as the roof of the long house."

In spite of his unhappiness, Atlin saw the great whale in his mind and felt the excitement of the story. "Did my father take up his harpoon?" he asked.

"He did," said Tokwit simply. "It was his time, the time he had long waited for. We came up easily behind the whale and he had not seen us. He was moving slowly and his great head was lifted high against the swells. When it drew down I steered the canoe in close and Nit-gass stood ready, high on the bow. The whale was so long that I had to look behind to watch the swing of his tail flukes. Perhaps that was why I did not see that his back was lifting as his head drew down. I gave the signal and the Chief struck him."

"Was it a strong thrust?" asked Atlin eagerly. "Did the harpoon find Kot-ske's heart?"

Tokwit shook his head. "No. It was a deep thrust, but high on the back, where there is too much bulk to go through. Nit-gass freed the harpoon shaft, but it was more difficult than usual and the canoe was slow in turning away. Nit-gass did not drop down from his place, but stood there watching, as he sometimes does. Then there was a shadow between me and the sun. I saw the whale's great tail sweep forward over the canoe, hurling water down on us. Nit-gass did not see it. It struck him squarely where he stood and threw him far out over the sea so that he looked like a shaman's doll against the sky."

"Was that all?" asked Atlin. "Could you not save him?"

"That was all. We threw the lines overboard and went quickly to where he had seen him fall, twenty or thirty canoe lengths away. But he was not there. We did not see him again, nor the whale, nor the lines, nor the floats, though we searched for a long time."

"So it is said that the great whale took my father to the village of the whale people?"

"Yes."

"And he will not come back?"

"Who knows?" said Tokwit. "No whale chief ever had greater power than your father. But if a blow of the whale's tail can break a canoe in little pieces, what must it do to a man?"

"I think I understand," said Atlin slowly. "If my father is in the village of the whale people he is no longer a man, but a Supernatural Being."

"Yes," said Tokwit. "You are the Hotsath Chief."

"What must I do?"

"There is little to be done now. Later there will be much. Tetacus and I will help you when that times comes."

"I do not like it here, where the people wail and moan and my mother is sad."

"Then go into the woods," said Tokwit. "Go to your father's shrine and make it your own."

Atlin gladly followed Tokwit's advice. He had eaten nothing since his father's death and he ate nothing now and took nothing with him. When he came to the pool below the falls he swam in it and rubbed himself with branches as his father had taught him, then crossed and climbed up to the shrine. It was evening and he meant to stay there all night.

When he reached the shrine he hesitated at the entrance as he had the first time Nit-gass brought him there. It seemed wrong to be there alone, without Nit-gass, and he half turned as though expecting to find his father smiling beside him. Then he felt a great loneliness, knowing that Nit-gass would never again step into the shrine and touch the things that were his. Because of it, the shrine seemed suddenly empty and without meaning. He stepped inside. The model of the sperm whale that had once seemed so vivid and powerful now seemed dusty and small, quite unconnected with the great whale Tokwit had described to him. The little harpooneer, standing in the canoe behind it, was no longer a brave man but a little bundle of dried rushes tied in the shape of a man. The carved figures of his whaling ancestors seemed to huddle against the wall of the shrine, as though ashamed to see him.

Again he looked behind him and all about him, apprehensively this time because he knew the place was powerful and it seemed all too likely that a spirit might appear and turn him back. Then he remembered Tokwit's words: "Go to your father's shrine and make it your own." He went on in and began to touch things, straightening the figures huddled against the outside wall, moving the sperm whale until he seemed more lively, picking up one of the paddlers that had fallen down in the canoe.

There were other things he had not noticed before—a dancer's rattles, several whaler's hats made of spruce roots, like those his father wore, and over in a corner a number of small boxes. He opened one and found two or three old harpoon heads and two very tiny rattles that he knew were spirit rattles of the kind people said were left on logs by the Supernatural Squirrel. In the next box were whale models that he recognised as Ma-ak, the grey whale, and the Soreface whale. He turned away from the boxes then and went to the broken harpoon shaft that leaned against the inside wall.

It was a heavy shaft, about fourteen feet long and made in three separate pieces carefully jointed and securely lashed together. It had broken in the middle of the heavy centre section, probably because of a flaw in the grain, but the carefully wrapped joints were still in place. Atlin did not know the story of the shaft, but he knew he wanted to put it together again and lift it in his hands. He laid the two pieces on the ground and found that the broken ends could be forced smoothly together; it would be a simple matter to bind them with nettle fibre or sinew and cover the binding with cherry bark so that it made a third joint. For the time being, this was enough and he replaced the broken pieces. As he did so, he noticed for the first time a long, slender piece of black stone, lying on the floor of the shrine close against the rock wall. The stone, which had been roughly shaped, was about eight feet long, tapering at each end from a thickness of four inches or more in the middle. Two bindings of red cedar bark, evenly spaced, marked it into three sections. It was easy to see that it represented a harpoon shaft.

For a moment Atlin hesitated. There was little doubt in his mind that it was an object of great power and he wondered if he dared touch it. Then he remembered Tokwit's words again and understood that this was the sort of thing they meant —to find the shaft, touch it, pick it up, were all part of making the shrine his own. He crouched down, put his hands on the stone and found he could not get a grip to lift it. He rolled it towards him, managed to get his hands under it, palms upward. It was very heavy, but in this way, balancing it carefully, he was able to lift it to the level of his shoulders and stand up with it. Standing so, he felt at once weak and powerful —weak because the strain of the lift took almost all his strength, powerful because he could feel the muscles of his shoulders and back and legs and arms hardening and swelling under the effort. Very carefully he lowered it again, set it gently on the floor and rolled it back into place.

The sun had set some while before and it was growing quite dark in the shrine. Once again Atlin felt fear and thought of going away to sleep down by the Forks or at the beach, anywhere but here. Then he felt a great sadness that hid fear quite away from him—a sadness for Nit-gass and for all those things in the shrine that would never know him again. He thought of the possibility that Nit-gass might come back as a spirit from the village of the Whale People and visit the shrine, but this did not change the sadness. The loss was Nit-gass himself, the Whale Chief, the man who laughed and joked, who came here to get ready for whaling, whose eyes lighted and whose body tensed at the very sight or sound of a whale, who dared drive his harpoon for the heart of any whale that swam; Nit-gass, whom men trusted and followed without question into the dangers and colossal effort of the whale hunt because he was a laughing man and unafraid.

It was quite dark now and Atlin lay down on the floor of the shrine to go to sleep. His head felt light and full of thoughts; the memory of Nit-gass made his heart strong and proud over its sadness; his body felt clean outside from bathing in the pool at the Forks and clean inside because it was so long since he had eaten. He went to sleep quickly and slept through the darkness. Towards dawn a little wind came up and a loose board in the roof of the shrine began to creak. Rain began to fall, at first lightly then more and more heavily until it was splashing and clattering all about the shrine. Atlin dreamed.

In his dream, a spirit came and told him to pick up the stone harpoon; he could not see its face or form, but he knew it was the whale spirit. Atlin went to the stone harpoon, reached down for it and tried to pick it up. His hands could not grip it and all his strength could not move it. The spirit was not angry, as Atlin expected it to be, but laughed the laugh of Nit-gass and said in his easy voice: "There is plenty of time. You will learn to lift it and then you will kill whales. When the harpoon is heavy it strikes to the heart of the whale." In the next moment he was beside Nit-gass in the bow of the canoe. They were far at sea and a strong westerly was making the canoe plunge and throw spray. Just ahead of them a whale rolled in the swells and the canoe was closing with it fast. Nit-gass handed him a harpoon and signalled him to take his place on the bow thwart, ready to strike. Nit-gass was laughing and his face and hair were streaming wet with spray.

Atlin took his place and the canoe closed. The whale was no longer a whale but a shark so enormous that he knew it could only be the Supernatural Shark. Atlin looked at his harpoon and saw at once that it was the broken shaft from the shrine, mended as he had planned to mend it. The canoe had closed now and Atlin was high over the shark's back, opposite the pectoral fin. He heard Tokwit's cry from the stern and struck. The harpoon shaft shattered in his hands as the blade entered and the broken pieces fell into the sea. Beside him Nit-gass laughed a great laugh and set a powerful hand on his shoulder. "It does not matter," he said. "You struck him well. You need only touch his tail and he is yours. Now." As he spoke the shark plunged down and his great tail swept past them. Atlin reached out a hand and felt the rasp of rough skin as he touched the shark's tail. Then his dream ended. He woke with one hand resting on a hump of bare rock that stuck up from the mossy floor of the shrine.

To Atlin the dream was not a dream but a meeting with spirits. He knew what he must do. Quickly he took four bundles of hemlock twigs from the rack and went down to the Forks to bathe, as daylight slowly grew through the heavy rain clouds.

13. Shark Point

THE REST of that summer after the death of Nit-gass passed quickly for Atlin. He found himself suddenly, in name at least, the principal chief of the tribe. Tetacus, Tokwit, Cumalik, the war chief, and other older men of the tribe advised him, but Atlin himself gave the orders and observed the ceremonial behaviour and duties of the principal chief.

Apart from this little was changed, but Tetacus and Tokwit encouraged him to go fishing and seal hunting at every opportunity, with or without Hinak. They also urged him to bathe regularly, to go without food quite often, to visit the shrine and to go through the woods and along the beaches in search of whatever spirits might come to him. Atlin had told them of his night at the shrine, of his vision of Nit-gass and the Supernatural Shark, and his discovery of the stone harpoon. Both men had considered the account very seriously. Tetacus said at last: "It is clear that you will one day be a great Whale Chief. The spirit of your father told you plainly the purpose of the stone harpoon. When you can lift it easily and hold it and practise your thrust with it as you would with a real harpoon, you will be strong enough to kill whales. The stone harpoon has been with us since the beginning of the Hotsath people. I have not heard that it has been lifted by a boy of your age before."

"I do not understand the Supernatural Shark," said Tokwit. "He is a tumanos for War Chiefs, not Whale Chiefs."

"It is plain he is not Atlin's tumanos," said Tetacus. "Atlin struck him with the harpoon that broke and almost killed my grandfather. There is some other meaning. I have heard that Nit-gass went sometimes to bathe in the Pool of the Supernatural Shark."

"I do not care for this thing," said Tokwit. "The Supernatural Shark means war."

"Atlin did not kill him. The shark did not kill them or break the canoe with his teeth. Nit-gass laughed. Atlin touched the Shark's tail to show that he had no fear of him. It is a strange thing, but I do not think it is evil."

Much more was said, then and at other times, which convinced Atlin that the dream was important to others as well as to himself. Tetacus explained to him that the meaning of supernatural occurrences, such as this one undoubtedly was, was not always clear at first but would gradually become clear as time went on. One had to remember the details carefully and be guided by them in future experiences.

The rest of that whaling season gave the Hotsath people little success. Only two more whales were brought to the beach and one of these was thin, with very little oil of poor quality. But the tribe was still wealthy from the successes of previous years under Nit-gass, and Tetacus gave a great winter dance and potlatch in Atlin's name. This was at once a memorial to Nit-gass and a formal recognition of the fact that Atlin had succeeded him as principal chief and was heir to all his rights and privileges. Even after the feasting, the people had food to last through the winter, though shortages began to appear in the stormy months before the herring spawning.

Atlin was now fourteen years old. He had changed greatly during the past year, growing taller and stronger, more nearly a man than a boy. The death of Nit-gass and the sudden responsibilities of the chieftainship had made him quieter and more serious than before. He knew that things were not going as well for the tribe as they had under Nit-gass and began to blame himself. One day he asked Tokwit: "When shall I be able to strike a whale?"

Tokwit looked hard at him, noticing how his chest had filled out and how the muscles of his arms and shoulders were building. "Perhaps next year," he said at last.

"Why not this year?"

"Have you lifted the stone harpoon yet?"

"Not as a man should," said Atlin. "No."

"Let that be your sign, as the spirit of your father told you It is not good to strike and lose the whale."

"Did my father kill the first whale he struck?"

"No," said Tokwit, "but the whale died. Tetacus was in a second canoe and struck the whale deeply. That is always how it is when a young chief brings in his first whale. But for you there is no one to strike surely. Tetacus is too old. I am crippled. Your uncle Kon-gass might do it, but he is never certain. The other whalers have not killed three whales among them in as many seasons."

"Why is it so bad if the first whale does not die?"

"It is not," said Tokwit. "But if the second and third also get away the people lose faith and say the Young Chief has no power. When this happens it is bad. If Nit-gass were here he might let you strike a whale this year, though you are still very young. But he is not here and you must grow your strength so that when you strike for the first time the people will know it is a man and a true Whale Chief who strikes."

"Will you tell me when it is time?"

"You will know when it is time," said Tokwit. "You will tell me and I will take you close to the whale. Go with Hinak in the sealing canoe. Hunt seals and porpoises and sea lions. Learn to feel the sea and understand it. Let your strength grow in you."

Atlin hid his disappointment, but he knew in his heart that Tokwit was right. He was not yet ready to stand up on the bow of the canoe and drive the heavy harpoon shaft with strength and certainty into the whale. He remembered his father's power, how he stood securely no matter how the canoe plunged and twisted, how his strong hands gripped the thick, smoke-darkened yew wood, how he swung it like a toy, grunted with the force of the thrust, laughed as the blade bit deep, withdrew the shaft, recovered and dropped down to the floor of the canoe in continuous movements of easy grace. All this was vivid and clear; he had tested himself against it in secret practice and knew he was not ready. But there was much more; the quick, sure commands after the whale was struck, the many decisions during the fight and, above all, the mysterious power by which the whaler controlled the whale's movements and protected his crew from its fury. Some of this power Atlin felt—from his dream at the shrine, from his bathing and fasting and the prayers he made to the Four Chiefs. But it was not yet as strong as it had to be.

The whaling was unsuccessful that summer. The weather was bad in the early part of the season and the canoes seldom got out. In June Kon-gass struck two whales which pulled free of the harpoon and got away; a third whale turned on the canoe and broke it, drowning one man, though a second canoe saved the others. In July Tetacus, old as he was, decided to go out with Tokwit and the rest of Nit-gass' crew.

When Atlin heard of this, he felt deeply ashamed. "My grandfather's strength is no longer great," he told Tokwit. "His bones hurt him. He cannot stand the cold. He might be killed."

Tokwit laughed. "He has an old man's cunning," he said. "Just as I have. As for the cold, we shall not go out far or stay out too long. He has power and we shall find the whales close in shore."

Atlin had an idea. "With his power in the canoe I could strike the whale for him."

Tokwit considered this. "No," he said at last. "You must find your own power first and the strength of your arms also. The Old Chief's power cannot carry too great a burden."

Disappointed, Atlin went back to his hunting with Hinak, taking his father's small, swift sealing canoe farther and farther from the village as his skill and confidence grew. Several times he harpooned porpoises and brought them back to the village. For this he was greatly praised by the older people, because it was well known that porpoises were difficult to approach; to strike them successfully meant that the hunter knew the sea, used his weapon skilfully and, above all, had powers not given to all men. Atlin was happy in all this, but it was not enough.

"Why is it that I must wait so long?" he asked Hinak.

"It is not long, Chief," said Hinak sensibly. "The people say it will be two years yet before you are ready to kill whales."

"If my Father were living, that would be all right. But the need is great already. The spirits must know this."

"You cannot hurry the spirits, except by prayers and bathing and going hungry. All this you are doing."

Then Atlin remembered his dream. "The Supernatural Shark!" he said excitedly. "I have not been to his place. Perhaps that is the meaning. Perhaps he is my tumanos."

"He is the tumanos of war chiefs," said Hinak doubtfully. "It is a fearful place. They say you must swim four times to get there and the sea reaches in to break you against the rocks each time."

"Who swims better than we do?" asked Atlin. "If war chiefs have found the Pool, we can. We will go."

They started out the next day, very early in the morning, for it was a long way. By full daylight they had reached Round Hill Point and clambered over the slippery rocks, past the tidal pools where they had often hunted sea urchins and starfish, past the ledges where the rockfish lay in hundreds. Now a great sweep of open beach lay ahead of them. In the distance they could see the round mass of Shark Island, the low line of Seal Rocks, and the bold cut of the bluffs on the point that reached out towards it. Somewhere under these the Pool lay, a fearful place, as deep as the bottom of the world, with dark water that foamed and hissed even on the stillest days and broke into whirlpools and surges as the great shark stirred his tail somewhere in the uneasy depths.

Atlin thought of all this as they began to run along the smooth, firm sand of the beach. It was a bright, still day and the sun already blazed fiercely on the open beach and on the smooth swells that heaved out of the ocean and rolled forward on to the sand. After a little both boys slowed down and began to walk. "It is hot," Hinak said. "We could go in the woods."

"It is too thick in there," Atlin told him. "It would take too long."

But even along the beach they went slowly in the heavy heat, stopping often to look at coon and deer tracks, searching for unusual pieces of wood in the drift. It was past noon before they came opposite Seal Rocks. Ahead of them the bluffs of Shark Point were sharp and clear and the Point itself seemed a low ledge of black rock against which the swells broke foaming even on that still day. High in the sky white clouds were moving from the west and when one crossed the face of the sun it made the sea and the bluffs and Shark Island seem suddenly threatening. "There is going to be a storm, Chief," Hinak said. "Perhaps we should turn back."

Atlin's heart had felt the same warning, but he wanted to go on as he had seldom wanted anything before. For the first time in many weeks he felt that he was doing something really important, that he could be coming close to the experience that would change his whole life and hurry the day when he could hunt whales as a whale chief in his own right." No," he said. "I must find the pool."

The beach was broken by great outcrops of black rock now and soon they came to the ledge under the bluffs and climbed on to it. Immediately they could see that it stretched ahead of them, tumbled and broken, for half a mile or more, curving round the always perpendicular face of the bluffs. The tide was at half flood. The sun blazed down again, but dark clouds were moving up and far out over the water they saw the black flurry of a little storm ahead of the main mass.

As they walked the ledge clouds closed over the sun and a cold wind met them. Suddenly the ledge ended in a narrow channel of water. It was heaving and violent, seamed and streaked with foam and bubbles, still hissing with the surge's withdrawal. It reached right back to the base of the bluffs and under them, into the rounded mouth of a cave. Beyond it the rock ledge went on, but there was no way around the channel. As they watched, a new surge came thundering up from the sea, racing and driving in plumes of white water against the steep black sides of the cleft. It swept past them, crashed into the cave, and buried its entrance in a leap of angry water that shattered on the face of the bluffs and hurled spray all about them.

"Is this what we must swim?" asked Hinak.

"Yes," said Atlin, "four times, Tokwit told me, each time farther than the last."

"You will not do it today, Chief."

"It will be easy," Atlin said. "There is time between the swells." But he knew there would not be much time.

A new surge came in, leaping and jostling against the rock walls, thundered past them and crashed again against the face of the bluffs. As its force spent Atlin began to climb down the rough rock wall of the cleft, directly behind the retreating

water. Hinak followed him. The water sucked down and down, then paused at last in hissing restlessness. Both boys plunged in. They struggled across, feeling the pull and twist of lesser whirls and currents against their bodies, slapped by the spray and tumble of the still broken surface. As they reached the far wall the roar of a new surge was already loud on the outer rocks. They scrambled out, finding toe holds and finger holds in the slippery surface of the wet rock. The new wave thundered in, leaping at them, battering them with spray, tearing at their legs and thighs as they clung to the rock. Somehow they held on, scrambled again and were safe on the far ledge.

Atlin looked down and saw blood on his thighs where the rocks and barnacles had cut them. He laughed and Hinak recognised the laugh of Nit-gass. They went on across the ledge and came to another channel, wider than the first. The sky was very dark now, with great black clouds over the sun, and suddenly the hail came hissing towards them over the angry water and across the rock ledges beyond the second channel. It lashed their bare bodies and drove them back until they were huddled together under the bluffs. A flash of lightning lit the rocks and the sea and the shadowy mass of Shark Island through the hail. Almost with it, a great roll of thunder burst on the air over them.

Both boys understood the warning and they looked at one another in fear. "The spirits are telling you to go back, Chief," Hinak said. "It is not your time to go to the Pool."

The words changed Atlin's fear to anger. For a moment he let himself believe they could go on. The wind drove past them and the hail lashed at their backs until tears came into their eyes from the sting of it and their flesh shivered from the cold. Atlin thought of the width of the next channel and the power of the rising sea. And there were two more channels, each wider than the one before it. He began to wonder whether they would be able to recross the first channel before the tide came up to trap them and batter them to death against the bluffs.

"It is not the spirits," he said at last. "But you are right. The time is bad."

Lightning flashed and thunder shook the air again. Hinak raised his eyes fearfully. "They speak again," he said. "They drive us away. You are not ready."

To his astonishment, Atlin laughed the laugh of Nit-gass again, his teeth gleaming and his eyes shining. "We will go back," he said, "but I shall come again soon."

He understood that he was not ready, though not altogether in the sense that Hinak meant. Before he came again he would bathe and fast and pray, to be ready for what he might find at the Pool itself. But for the rest, the crossing of the angry channels to find the Pool, it was only necessary to choose a calm day or, better still, a calm night.

They turned back with the hail still hammering on them, lightning flashing and thunder roaring. The surge was higher and fiercer in the channel than before, but they plunged in boldly behind it and crossed swiftly. Again they were clinging to the far wall as the fierce water came back, but this time it reached to their chests and played about their shoulders, battering at their bodies, tearing at the grip of their fingers and feet. Suddenly Hinak lost his grip. At his cry Atlin reached out and grabbed his wrist, holding him against the fierce uneven pull of the water that would have hurled him on to his death against the rock wall of the bluffs. For a moment the surge hung about them in turbulent pause, then it drew back almost as powerfully as it had stormed in. Hinak regained his grip on the broken face of the rock and they climbed out together.

Ten minutes later the storm had passed beyond them, the sun was out and they were running over the sand in the cleared air. In spite of his disappointment, Atlin's heart was light. Holding Hinak against the surge, he had felt such a strength in his arms and body as he had never known before. Perhaps the Thunderbird of the high mountains had sent the warning to turn back. But the thundering sea itself had roared equally. He remembered the words of his father Nit-gass: "A man should have power before he goes to such places." For the first time he felt that the power was very close to him.

14. *The Tumanos*

DURING the rest of that season only two whales were brought
into the Hotsath beach—one killed by Tetacus, one by Kon-
gass. Very late in the season Tetacus killed another whale,
but it took the canoe far out to sea before it died. As they were
towing the carcass back towards shore a heavy storm came up
and after struggling through the night the canoe had to cut
loose. When the storm died down many canoes went out from
the village to search for the dead whale, but they could not
find it. Tetacus was sick for several days from the wet and
cold of the long struggle with the whale and Tokwit was afraid
he might die, blaming himself for not persuading the old man
to turn back sooner.

The stormy weather of spring and summer had reduced the
catches of halibut fishermen and seal hunters. The salmon runs
had been good and the fishing well-timed, but the Hotsath
territory had only two small salmon streams and the salmon
catch was only a small part of the year's food supply. There
was little feasting in the Hotsath village that winter and by
January the people were hungry. Heavy snows fell early in the
month and stormy seas still held the canoes on shore. The people
turned to the beaches in search of clams, mussels, octopus,
crabs, anything they could find.

Again Atlin felt ashamed that he could not do more. Remembering the tales of old hunters, he persuaded Hagilt to come with him and Hinak to the elk meadows far up the Hotsath River. It was a hard journey from the dog salmon village at the mouth of the river through ever deepening snow and Hagilt protested that it was a foolish venture for whalers.

"Did not my father hunt elk in the deep snow?" asked Atlin. "And did you not go with him to hold his cloak while he ran them down?"

"That is all true enough, Chief," said Hagilt. "But we were very young men then. The Chief, your father, was always impatient to hunt something when he was stormbound."

"So am I," said Atlin.

"Nit-gass did not hunt elk to feed his people. He wanted the hide and the bone and the sinew more than the meat. That is for the woods people along the big river at the head of the inlet. They know nothing of whales or seals and think a halibut is a supernatural fish because it has both eyes on one side of its head."

Both Atlin and Hinak laughed at this, for it was an old joke. But Atlin said seriously: "We have little of whale or seal, or halibut either. You are as gloomy as Shiyus."

They found the elk browsing on the red osier at the edge of the meadows. Running on clumsy snowshoes, they singled out one from the herd and chased it through the deep snow until they brought it to bay in floundering terror. Atlin closed and drove his pointed yew wood spear to the heart, then watched the red blood stain the snow while his chest heaved painfully from the running.

The elk had scattered and were difficult to approach a second time. It was nightfall before they killed another. They slept in the snow and hunted again the next morning, and again it was difficult. Atlin killed one more, a small and sickly cow, but they could find no others.

"You have done well enough," said Hagilt, "but they will not come back again until the man smell is gone. And we cannot follow them because they will travel faster than we can through the woods."

They butchered the dead animals, folded the meat in the hides and hung it in the trees to keep it from the wolverines and mountain lions.

"It will fill the people's bellies for a day or two," said Hagilt. "But it is a long way to carry it to the canoes. And it would not be so easy another time."

Atlin knew he was right, but he said: "With more hunters we could kill more."

"We have no land hunters, Chief," said Hagilt. "Nit-gass hunted the elk occasionally and now you have hunted them. It is good that you have done so, but you had better go back to the shrine and learn to lift the stone harpoon."

"Do you think I can learn before it is time to hunt whales again?"

"Yes," answered Hagilt without hesitation. "You are strong already. The whale hunter's heart is in you. You bathe as a whaler should, through every waxing moon. You can go without food for days together. Very soon now you will find your tumanos."

February was still stormy and there was little that Tetacus or Tokwit or Atlin could do except urge the people to go out and search the beaches and send the fishermen into Kashutl Inlet on the calmer days to fish for spring salmon and watch for the herring. Word came to the village that a great whale had drifted on to the Tsitikat beach and that Eskowit was claiming that he had found the power of Nit-gass and added it to his own.

"Why should he say that?" Atlin asked Tokwit.

"He says that the body of Nit-gass washed up on his beach and he made great magic with it."

Atlin's heart chilled. "Do you believe this?"

"No," said Tokwit. "Perhaps he found some other body. But not Nit-gass. He is with the Whale People."

"How did he make the magic?"

"I do not know. It is said that Eskowit takes the body of a man who has power and drives a stake through the back of his neck so that it comes out through his mouth. Then he drives a hollow tube through the wound, sets the body facing out to sea and calls through the tube for the whales to drift to his beaches. It is strong magic."

"If he did that to my father," Atlin said. "I will kill him."

"No," said Tokwit. "I have told you it was not your father."

"If he says he did it to my father, I will kill him."

"No," said Tokwit. "He says it only to make himself big and make you small. There are better ways than killing him."

"What ways?" asked Atlin.

"You will find them. It is not good to talk of killing. Make yourself a Whale Chief like Nit-gass and you will find a way."

It was at the time of the waxing moon in February that Atlin heard these things. He had been bathing regularly in the sea, finding sheltered places where the surf did not beat too powerfully. Now he fasted four full days and nights and deliberately turned away from the sea, into the woods, following the trails of the wild animals. He came at last to the Forks of the Kamiss River, swam across and climbed up to the shrine. His body felt strong and eager, his head was full of light and brilliant thoughts. At the shrine he prayed to the Four Chiefs, then went at once to the stone harpoon. He crouched in front of it, set his hands, palms down, on the bindings, gripped and lifted the harpoon for the first time. He straightened his legs under the weight, feeling it carefully, lifting it against his chest. For several moments he stood, struggling to make himself turn the harpoon into its thrusting position. His legs trembled and his body began to sweat, but he still could not turn the harpoon. Somehow he knew that if he did so his grip would fail, the harpoon would slip away and shatter on the floor of the shrine. Instead, he set his feet more firmly and began to lift the harpoon above his head to the full reach of his arms. He lifted it again and again, balancing it horizontally on his palms, struggling until his arms grew tired and the sweat poured off him. At last he crouched down again, gripped firmly and gently lowered the shaft back to its place on the floor of the shrine. His grip did not fail him.

He was so exhausted that his arms trembled, the muscles of his shoulders and belly quivered and his chest heaved. But the spirit that was driving him was not stilled and he went at once to bathe at the Forks. He swam the four circuits of the pool as Nit-gass had taught him, rubbing himself with hemlock branches each time until the blood came to the surface of his skin. After the fourth circuit and the fourth rubbing, he flung himself on the bear robe he had left at the edge of the pool. Lying there it seemed to him that he had no body, but only a head that could feel arms and legs and chest of fire, dancing, expanding as heat waves over the hot beach on a summer's day.

As he lay there he heard a bird call, very close. He knew it was a spirit call and sat up. At the edge of the water, almost under his feet, a little dark grey bird stood on a rock and bobbed up and down. The bird called again, fluttered a few feet and perched on another rock. From there it walked into the water, swam a little way, then dived. Atlin followed its movements easily as it darted this way and that. Then he saw that it was walking on the bottom as easily as it had walked on dry land. It bobbed to the surface with a tiny fish struggling in its beak. It walked up on to the rock again, shook itself, swallowed the fish, bobbed several times and uttered its cry. Then it flew off upstream, very close to the water, to disappear under the falls. Atlin understood at once that this was Gakatas, the little whale bird, that had been his Father's tumanos.

Gakatas had taken the form of this little freshwater bird, to come to the Pool at the Forks and show that it had now become his tumanos. He was exhausted now and frightened, because he knew he had seen a spirit. He could not move from where he was, but lay back again and felt the fire running in his body again. After a long while he stood up, stretched himself, then turned and ran off into the woods, leaving the bear robe at the edge of the pool.

When he came to himself, Atlin was lying on his own bed in the long house. He tried to move and found that he was bound to the bed by a strong rope across his chest. Witamis, the son of the war chief, and another young man were holding his arms. He tried to shake them off, then sighed deeply and lay back. He saw Tetacus standing over him.

"Are you well again, Chief?" the old man asked. "Have you come back to us?"

"Yes, Grandfather," Atlin said. "I am well."

Tetacus signalled and the rope was freed from about his chest, though the two young men still held his arms.

"You have brought back great power," Tetacus said. "We were afraid for you. But you have found your tumanos."

Atlin remembered the little bird at the pool. "Yes," he said, "I have found it. It was also the tumanos of my Father, Nit-gass. It came to me in another form, but it was the same."

"You have already told us these things," said Tetacus. "When the spirit power was strong in you. It is good that you remember them clearly now."

15. *The Sea Lion*

MARCH, the herring spawn month, was still stormy, but there were spells of calmer weather and from time to time the seal hunters were able to go out and bring in a few seals. Atlin and Hinak went out each time and brought in their share, though Atlin was impatient because they did not kill more. The people were still hungry, living from day to day on what came into the village.

On one sealing trip Atlin hunted well beyond Shark Island, beyond the main halibut bank towards Hotsath Island and the mouth of Tsitikat Inlet, at the extreme northern end of Hotsath territory. On the ocean side of Hotsath Island they came on a small herd of sea lions. Atlin harpooned one, which immediately dived and ran hard, tearing the line through his hands so fast that he could barely ease the strain safely on to the thwart. The canoe began to tear through the water and the sea lion surfaced, thrashing ponderously. As he dived again, the harpoon head pulled free. Though they hunted hard through the rest of the day, they could not come close to the herd again.

Generally the Hotsath people did not hunt sea lions very vigorously because they much preferred the seal blubber. But the sea lions were six or eight times as large as the seals, some of the big males weighing nearly a ton, and it seemed to Atlin that he should try to find the herd again and kill one or more of them. He remembered that his father had had two or three special harpoon heads, made like whaling heads with a mussel shell blade, but considerably smaller. Next time they went out, he took one of these, with a stronger line and two of the sealskin whaling floats. Instead of tying the end of the line to the bow thwart, he tied it to an inflated float, keeping the second float as a spare in case there should be a chance to strike a second animal before the first was killed.

They started long before daylight, over a sea that was uneasily calm, with a breeze just stirring from the south. Hinak did not trust the weather. "It will storm before night," he said.

Atlin agreed with him, but he said only: "It is a long time before night."

The dawn was grey, with a drifting fog that completely enclosed them at one moment then, seconds later, lifted to reveal the line of Hotsath Island and closed down again. The sea was calm, but restless, heaving in short swells that seemed to have no regular pattern. It was a good morning for hunting and Atlin told Hinak to hold well in towards the island.

Once they saw a seal, but could not come close and lost him in the fog. Then, as the fog lifted, they saw the sea lions playing half a mile or more away. The fog came down again and they paddled swiftly but with careful, silent strokes towards the herd.

When he thought they were close, Atlin silently set down his paddle and picked up his harpoon. He was watching the water as far ahead as he could see, at the edge of the fog that rimmed them. The big bull surfaced almost under the bow and had already begun his dive as Atlin swung his harpoon from the throwing position and plunged it into him. The coiled line leapt out, sliding away into the grey sea. Then a kink caught under a thwart and wrenched the canoe over so sharply that Atlin was thrown into the water before he knew what had happened. He felt the line rasp over his back as he came up, turned, grabbed it and was at once towed under. He held on as long as he could, delighting in the rush of water past his body and the pressure of it on his ears and head. Then he let go and came up in time to see Hinak throw the float overboard and turn the canoe towards him. He climbed aboard and shook himself, laughing with excitement and pleasure as he saw Hinak's shocked face.

"Quick," he said. "Keep after the float before we lose it in the fog."

"Why did you hang on to the rope, Chief?" said Hinak reprovingly. "If you had tangled in it he would have drowned you."

"He is not like a whale. The drag of a man can slow him."

Ahead of them, the sea lion came up with a bellow and began to travel at the surface, faster than before, dragging the float.

"Did you strike him deep?" asked Hinak.

"Deep enough to hold, but not to the heart. I did not expect him where he was."

"He will fight long then."

The breeze was freshening now and the fog was lifting. Atlin saw that they were nearly at the north end of Hotsath Island and the sea lion was travelling due north, towards the mouth of Tsitikat Inlet.

"We had better catch up and kill him," Atlin said, "before he goes too far."

The sea lion had slowed and they recovered the float without much difficulty. But strain as he would, Atlin could gain little on the rope as the great beast towed them steadily northward, still travelling on the surface with a graceful ease that seemed untiring. The breeze was still picking up and Hinak said: "It will be hard to tow him back."

"If it is too hard we will cut him up in the water and load him in the canoe."

But an hour passed and it seemed they were still no closer to the kill. Several times Atlin had recovered a good deal of line, only to have it torn out through his hands again. The sea lion still held northwards and the freshening breeze drifted them in the same direction. Atlin remembered that the currents from everywhere north of the main halibut bank set towards the Tsitikat beaches. In the distance he could already see the line of Eskowit's village close under the dark woods. His muscles ached and his hands were sore and cramped, but he strained and heaved until the tiring sea lion was within a few feet of the canoe. The great broad back and wrinkled neck seemed enormous and he wondered if his heavy sealing club would be enough to kill it. Then the sea lion surged away again, taking out all the line he had recovered.

Behind him, Hinak said quietly: "There's a canoe coming out from the village. Perhaps they will help."

Atlin looked up sharply. The canoe was a small one with only two men in it, approaching swiftly. Well behind it were two others, larger. "We don't need help," said Atlin angrily. "Let them catch their own sea lions."

The sea lion was plainly tiring now and he recovered line fairly easily. The Tsitikat canoe drew close and a man stood up in the bow.

"What have you caught, Chief?" he shouted.

"A great bull sea lion," said Atlin. Then he added, none too willingly. "I will give you his flippers if you will help me."

The Tsitikat laughed. "Perhaps he has caught you."

"They did not come to help," said Hinak softly. "Perhaps they have come to kill us."

Atlin considered the possibility. Sometimes wars between the tribes started in this way, with the slaughter of an isolated hunting party. But there was no real cause for war between the Tsitikats and the Hotsaths. "No," he said. "But they do not mean us well."

The other two canoes were close now and Atlin recognised Eskowit standing in the bow of the first one. The sea lion was

plainly tiring and the canoe was again within a few feet of it. Then the great beast shook himself, bellowed in fear and anger and dived straight down. Eskowit laughed loudly.

"You are having trouble, Chief. You have no control over that thing. It is drifting in my waters."

"He is my catch," said Atlin boldly. "I harpooned him off Hotsath Island many hours ago."

Again Eskowit laughed. "He is mine now. Everything that drifts in my waters is mine. You know the laws, Chief."

The sea lion had surfaced again. It was very tired now. Atlin made no move to recover line, but simply held the strain, playing for time.

"The wind is coming up," said Eskowit. "But you do not have to worry, Chief. When you kill him we will take him off your hands."

"Cut the line," said Hinak quietly. "Don't let them take him."

Atlin had already considered this, but he had no wish to lose his father's harpoon head. Eskowit's canoes were still standing well off, as though to make it clear they would give no help. Atlin knew that the sea lion's struggles had torn the harpoon head from much of its hold in the flesh and blubber and that it was now only a little way under the skin, though still deep enough to hold the tired animal. He felt a bitter hatred of Eskowit, the more bitter because he knew that his claim had some shadow of right; the waters were his, though the sea lion was capture, not drift.

"You should be glad, Chief," said Eskowit tauntingly. "It is your father's power that has brought you here, as it brought me the dead whale with your grandfather's harpoon last year."

Atlin had begun to recover line, but he straightened and looked squarely at Eskowit. "You lie, Chief," he said. "My father's power brought live whales to his people, not rotten carcasses that are only fit for dogs to eat."

Eskowit laughed. "Yet the Hotsath people are hungry, while the Tsitikats have feasting and full bellies."

The sea lion was close to the canoe now and seemed to have lost its will to fight. The wound from the harpoon thrust was on the side nearest the canoe; it was a wide wound, torn by the pull of the line. Atlin heaved mightily and brought it as close to him as he could. He dared not reach for his knife, but dropped suddenly to his knees, holding the line hard against the gunwale of the canoe with his left hand while he plunged his right hand into the wound. His fingers followed the line, probing into the blubber, found the barbs close under the hide and gripped them firmly. In the same moment he released the strain on the line so that the canoe lifted and the sea lion's weight pulled his hand free with the harpoon head securely held in it. He dropped the harpoon head and slapped his bloody hand against the broad, dun-coloured back of the sea-lion. The great beast lay for a moment without moving and Atlin shouted to it: "Go, you are free."

As though responding to the urgent voice, the sea lion rolled over and dived. Atlin stood up, watching the swirling water and the bubbles of the dive. There were shouts from the Tsitikat canoes.

Atlin looked up at Eskowit. "There is your drift, Chief. I have given it to you. If you have the power of Nit-gass, you will gather it without trouble."

He picked up his paddle and swung the canoe away, into the rising wind. "Let us go back," he told Hinak. "There is not much time."

Behind them, the Tistikat canoes had scattered over the water, watching for the sea lion to surface again. Hinak watched them over his shoulder. "What if they find him?" he asked.

Atlin laughed. "They will not. He will surface no more than his nostrils to breathe. And very soon the wind will drive them in. The power of Eskowit does not reach very far."

16. The Pool

WHEN HE released the sea lion and turned away from Eskowit, Atlin had no sense of triumph, only of loss. But word of the meeting and its outcome spread rapidly among the tribes and brought him great credit. Tetacus praised him freely.

"You have the way of a great chief," he said. "It is born in you and now that you have found your tumanos it comes out so that all men can see it."

"But he forced me to turn the sea lion loose," said Atlin. "I did not want to do it. And he was right by the law; we were in his waters."

"True," agreed Tetacus. "But to be great, a chief must be generous. Eskowit was small. He thought it would be easy to take the sea lion from you and make a joke of you. Instead, you made a joke of him, yet you obeyed the law as it is between chiefs."

"He was angry. Do you think he will try to do us harm?"

"There was no insult. The law was obeyed. I do not think his people would follow him to make war. But it is well to be on our guard. We will post guards on the village at night and tell the people not to go beyond the main halibut banks for a little while."

April came with gentler weather. The herring spawn was

successfully gathered and the halibut fishermen began to come in with good catches of the huge, white-bellied flatfish. Families began to visit from tribe to tribe and word soon came that Eskowit had called a council after the affair of the sea lion, but had found little support for his idea of retaliation against the Hotsath people. The memory of the greatness and generosity of Nit-gass was still fresh in the minds of all the tribes and there was no store of hatred on which to build enthusiasm for war. Even so, Tetacus took the matter seriously, for he knew that the Hotsath people were weak and open to attack and would be until Atlin reached his full stature as chief. He knew also how quickly ambition and jealousy could be used to stir a tribe to attack if there seemed hope of surprise or an easy victory.

"It is not good that there should be ill feeling between Chiefs," he told Atlin. "You must reach an understanding with Chief Eskowit."

"How can I?" asked Atlin, "when he says he has my Father's power?"

"He knows it is not so. When you become a Whale chief and bring whales to the beach everyone will know it is not so."

"How will that make understanding between us?"

"By itself it will not," said Tetacus. "But soon you will need a wife. Chief Eskowit has daughters. There has not been an important marriage between the Hotsath and the Tsitikats for many years."

The idea was not altogether new to Atlin. His mother had spoken to him several times of marriage. She herself was the daughter of a Kashutl chief, while his grandmother, the wife of Tetacus, was a Nitinat. He knew also that such marriages were used to open the way for understanding and to keep peace among the tribes.

"What you say is wise, Hawil," he said. "But first I must

become the whale chief in truth so that I shall not be a poor man begging for the daughter of a wealthy chief."

Tetacus laughed. "You have wealth enough," he said. "But what you say is true. Go and lift the stone harpoon. You are ready."

Atlin had been to the shrine only a few days earlier and had lifted the stone harpoon. It was easy for him now and he could swing it in his hands and even turn it as though to make a thrust, but he was still afraid it might break from his grip and shatter on the floor of the shrine. He believed that this was because he had still not been to the Pool of the Supernatural Shark, and he was now more than ever determined to do so. He watched weather and tide anxiously through the waxing moon of April and at last found a dead calm with a tide that would give them several hours to reach the pool and return from it. He woke Hinak and they started at once.

The young moon was bright when they started. The gentle sea and the sea mists were moving silver under it. The wet black rocks and streaming sea-weeds of Round Hill Point shone in a thousand points of light and the great sweep of sand beach beyond was shadowless and unmarked, with wisps and trails of mist that lifted barely knee high before they were lost in the clear air. Hinak, less used to the beaches at night than Atlin, was nervous and started violently when a deer, heavy with fawn, leapt away from their coming and disappeared into the woods.

"If I were a spirit," he said, "I would choose a night like this to move."

"It is not easy to see spirits," said Atlin seriously. "I have bathed here a hundred nights and not seen one, though I have heard them."

"There will be spirits at the Pool," said Hinak. "I do not much want to go there, even with you."

"The old people say spirits do not show themselves as they

did in the olden days. You have only to search for them to know the truth of that."

"But in such places you feel them close to you. That is enough. You are a chief and have your tumanos to protect you. I have nothing."

"You are with me," said Atlin. "It is the will of the Supernatural Shark that I go to his place or he would not have showed himself in my dream. Nothing evil will happen to us. You will see."

They were running easily on the hard-packed sand, breathing the sea mists, their shadows long in the moonlight. Only a tiny part of Hinak's fear touched Atlin; he felt sure that they would reach the Pool this time, that he would bathe there as he had long meant to and that he would be ready for anything strange or fearful that might happen. He had learned in the past years that the strange and fearful things that did happen were neither so strange nor so fearful as the imagination had supposed they would be and, more important, that neither his body nor his mind was likely to fail him at the moment of encounter.

The moon was well down towards the horizon when they came to the rock ledges and the first channel. The tide was still well down and the surge from the calm sea was so gentle that it did not break over the mouth of the cave but plunged into it with a rolling hiss that faded to a distant sigh before the withdrawal. The second channel was shielded from the direct light of the moon by the bulk of Shark Island and it was difficult to judge the surges, but they swam it safely and climbed out over the trailing slippery seaweeds and the levels of mussels and barnacles to the next ledge. The third channel was wider and the returning surge caught them when they were almost across. It was gentle but still powerful and its force rushed them through the darkness at terrifying speed towards the unknown face of the bluffs. Atlin reached the far wall and found a hold. He felt Hinak's body brush past him, gripped him and held him easily against the smooth flow. They scrambled out, rasping their bodies against the barnacles crusted on the rock.

Atlin's mind was so firmly set on reaching the Pool that he did not notice Hinak's trembling until they came to the last channel.

"What is it?" he asked. "Are you hurt?"

"The moon has left us, Chief," Hinak's voice was strained with terror. "It is a bad sign. I am afraid some evil thing will happen."

"It is only behind the island," Atlin was studying the channel intently, because it was very wide. "When we come to the Pool it will be with us again."

"Some evil is close to us," Hinak said. "I can feel it."

"I do not feel any evil," Atlin said calmly. "And we can cross easily. The channel is so wide that the surge has no force. But stay here if you are afraid. I will go alone."

"No, Chief, if you go, I go with you."

"Why? You would be safe here and if I do not come soon you can cross the channels and wait for me on the beach."

"You know I cannot. If I went back to the village without you they would kill me."

"You are my brother," said Atlin. "No one would harm you." But he knew at once that this was not true. Any slave who returned without his chief would be killed. "You were not afraid of dying when Eskowit's canoes were all about us," he said.

"We were together. I could have served you then."

"Then serve me now. It is only a little way farther. No one is going to die."

They crossed together, swimming side by side in the darkness, speaking occasionally to keep touch. As they climbed out on the far side Atlin knew that Hinak's courage had returned. His own had grown and strengthened as he tested it against

Hinak's fears. What they would find at the Pool he did not know; but whatever it might be he knew his power would meet it.

Beyond the last channel the black rock of Shark Point was tumbled and broken by the wear of the sea and they found themselves climbing rather than walking. At one point they came down on to a tiny sand beach with a bay in front of it fed by a narrow surge channel completely hidden by its high rock walls and for a moment Atlin thought they had found the Pool. They climbed away from it, over another ridge folded tightly under the steep bluffs and the Pool was there before them, unmistakeable in the long light of the setting moon that now slipped past Shark Island. Silently they climbed down to it and Atlin felt his throat dry and his heart beating hard.

A great curve in the bluffs made the inland wall of the Pool. There was no beach, nor even any sign of a ledge, but simply the sheer, smooth rock climbing directly out of the water. The ridge they were standing on also broke off abruptly into the dark water and seemed to continue the curve of the bluffs until it broke into a line of gaunt rocks spaced like sentinels and fencing in the Pool's seaward curve until their meeting with the ridge on the far side that curved into the bluffs again. Beyond the sentinel fence were more rocks and rocky islets of every shape and size against which even that calm and lazy sea broke with an unceasing stir of troubled water. The Pool itself, troubled by the conflicting flow of surges from the channels between the spaced rocks that fenced it, was uneasy and broken, forever slapping and washing against its rock walls, recoiling, gathering into little peaks of water, to rush forward and strike again.

Looking at the place, Atlin readily understood why the Hotsath people said that no canoe could ever come there. On such a night as this it might be possible to steer safely in amongst the rocks. But the least rise of wind, the smallest increase in the

swells, would trap the canoe and its people into certain destruction against the face of the bluffs or the rock walls of the en-
circling ridges.

Hinak shivered. "What are you going to do?" he asked in a
whisper.

"I shall bathe," said Atlin. He also spoke in a whisper.
"Exactly as I always do. I shall swim four times."

He began to walk along the ridge towards the point where it
met the water. He was moving slowly and heavily now, as
whalers always did when they followed their rituals. Just short
of the point, at a place where he could go easily down into the
water, he stopped and began to gather bundles of seaweed for
the rubbing. Suddenly Hinak gripped his arm. "Look," he
whispered tensely. "Look, Chief. The Shark."

Atlin straightened and looked into the Pool. "There,"
Hinak pointed. "There it is again."

Atlin saw the lazy movement of a great dorsal fin against the
disturbed surface of the Pool, moving very slowly towards
them. Behind it the backward curving upper lobe of the tail
also broke the surface. The great shark came lazily below them,
swung gracefully to face the inflow of the sea surges and was
still. Its back was awash and the lines of its enormous body were
perfectly clear in the last long rays of the moon. Atlin had felt
his face and neck prickle with fear and fear had grown into
terror at the shark's approach. But now the slow and lazy
movement, the familiar shape had somehow matched his mood
and reassured him. Supernatural or no, he knew that this was
his shark, the shark of his dream. It was not hostile, but friendly.
He knew what to do.

While Hinak stood rooted in horror, he moved slowly down
the rocks and slid silently into the water a few feet behind the
shark. Still silently and stealthily, he swam forward, then
reached up and touched the tail. The shark moved very slightly,
then was still again. Atlin gripped the forward edge of the fin,

slid his hand down along the rough surface and gripped more firmly.

"Shark," he said loudly. "I have touched you now as I did in my dream. I know you will not hurt me or break my canoe when I go to sea. Watch my canoe, Shark, so that the whales do not break it." The shark had begun to move, as though aware of him, though still very slowly. "You are going now, Shark," Atlin said, his voice still strong. "When you visit the village of the whale people, tell them that the son of Nit-gass and his people are waiting to welcome them and do them honour."

He loosed his grip and the shark drew away, still slowly. Behind him, Atlin dived lazily, rolled up and blew with the grey whales's spout. Absorbed in his terror, enclosed by the inevitable bond between himself and the actors in the Pool below him, Hinak crouched on the rocks, seeing only the moving bodies among the dancing lights and shadows of the broken water. Atlin dived again, rolled and spouted, dived again in slow completion of his ritual circle. Beyond him the shark also circled, swinging his forty-feet body in a majestic sweep that seemed scarcely movement at all, though it placed him at last with his head directly towards Atlin and about twenty feet from him. Hinak tried to shout a warning, but no sound came from his throat. Atlin dived and spouted a fourth time, swung in and climbed slowly out of the water. Without even glancing at Hinak, he began to rub his body with seaweed from the pile he had gathered.

Hinak found his voice. "It is him, Chief," he said softly and urgently. "The Breaker of Canoes. The Supernatural Shark."

A spirit of exaltation had gripped Atlin. He felt power such as he had never known, a certainty in all his actions that left him without fear or doubt. He heard Hinak's words from a great way off and felt laughter in his chest and belly because they were so wrong. "This one?" he said. "The Breaker of Canoes? Look at his mouth. It could scarcely crush a paddle. It is not him, but his child."

"Do not go back," Hinak begged. "Do not go back."

But Atlin had already slipped into the water again and began his second circle. On his hand he could still feel the roughness of the shark's skin, as he had felt it in his dream. Now it seemed that the shark was standing guard over him, a benevolent, protective watch that reduced the dangers and terrors of the Pool to nothing. When he made the fourth circle the moon had gone below the horizon, but the shark was still in its place. As he dragged himself out over the barnacled rocks for the last time, weary but still elated, he thought the faint light from the sky showed him the twin triangles of tail and dorsal fin slowly moving away across the surface of the Pool.

17. The New Whale Chief

A FEW DAYS after the visit to the Pool, Tetacus found Atlin working spruce gum into the wrapping of a new harpoon head. For several moments he watched in silence, then he said casually: "It is almost time to look for whales again, Chief."

"Yes, Grandfather," Atlin agreed cautiously. "There is much to be done."

"Have you spoken to Tokwit yet?"

Atlin looked up at his grandfather in surprise. "No," he said. "I have not yet lifted the stone harpoon."

"That is true," said Tetacus, "Yet you know you can."

Again Atlin was surprised. He did know. He had known ever since he had touched the tail of the Shark in the Pool. It was only because he was so certain in his mind that he had not bothered to go up to the Shrine. Tetacus went on: "You are different now. You have been changing all winter long, but mostly in the last few days. Now you are a man of full power. The people can feel it in you. I can feel it."

Atlin stood up, his face flushed with pleasure. He set his shoulders and tightened the muscles of his arms and heavy chest. "Yes," he said. "I can feel the strength all through me. Yet I have done very little."

"It is true you have not yet killed a whale. But you have done much and it shows in you. Now you must tell Tokwit to get the crew together and make sure the canoe is ready."

"Before I have been to the Shrine?"

"There will be time for that. But there is much else to be done."

In spite of the strength and power he felt within himself, Atlin went reluctantly in search of Tokwit. It seemed strange that he, who had never taken any real part in the killing of a whale, should be the one to warn the crew to prepare themselves and the canoe to be made ready. Yet something inside him knew that even this was right and necessary.

He found Tokwit with Solmic, the canoe maker, an old grey-haired man with long arms, bent knees and a heavily lined face. They were talking together, pointing at the two whaling canoes that had once belonged to Nit-gass and now belonged to Atlin.

"It is good that you have come, Hawil," said Tokwit.

"My grandfather said that I must come and tell you I am ready to strike a whale."

"I know, I know," said Tokwit, still studying the canoes. "But which canoe will you take? This was Nit-gass' favourite—the one from which he struck the sperm whale. It is strong and quick and has a high prow, which he liked. The other is older, but it is good too and he killed many whales from it."

"The old one will be better at first," said Atlin without hesitation. "If the whale should break it because I do not strike his heart it will not matter so much."

Old Solmic laughed. "You are right, Hawil. It is the young chiefs who break canoes, but the old ones who are rich enough to pay for them. We will get the old one ready for you. It must be scorched and polished."

Atlin thanked the old man and he and Tokwit walked slowly away together. "How did you know I was ready?" asked Atlin.

"I have known for a long time that you would be ready this year. But when I heard you had touched the tail of the shark, I knew the time had come."

"It was not the Supernatural Shark."

"It was in his Pool."

"I have seen others like it, and almost as big. It was like a basking shark, and lazy like they are."

"It does not matter," answered Tokwit. "No man would go into the Pool when it was there, much less touch it, unless he had great power."

"I have not swung the stone harpoon."

"It does not matter," answered Tokwit again. "Whenever you choose you will do so. If the weather is good we can go out in about two weeks. We will tell the crews to get ready."

"Can Hinak go with us? He is a good paddler."

"I thought you would want him. But it would not be good the first time. Wait until you have killed some whales. The fourth paddler is old. His shoulders and knees hurt him. Soon he will not want to go out."

When he left Tokwit that morning, it seemed to Atlin that two weeks would never pass. But the days were full days. Tokwit made him check every stage of the preparations, showing him how to test the lines and floats, the line baskets, the water boxes and food boxes, warning him that even small things like bailers and mats were important and could at times make the difference between living and dying. "It is said that a Chief does not work," Tokwit told him. "But a Chief must know. Nit-gass knew. There was nothing he could not do, even women's work, if he had to. So he knew when the work was well done or ill done and he did not lose whales because the lines broke or the canoe was not ready."

When the first sliver of moon showed in May, Atlin began bathing again. After bathing four nights in succession from the rocks of Round Hill Point he went to the shrine and lifted the stone harpoon. His grip held it firmly and he swung it as he chose, delighting in the stretch and pull of his muscles, the easy play of his body. He lifted and swung it and thrust it again and again until the sweat started all over him. Then he set it down in its place and went to straighten the figure of the whaler in the model canoe. He took down the model of the sperm whale and set up a model of Ma-ak, the grey whale, in its place. Then he prayed to the Four Chiefs, asking for good weather, promising that he would treat the grey whale with honour if it would be the first to take his harpoon. Even in this he protected himself a little, offering to do the same for a sore-face or even a killer whale if one of these should be the first.

The weather, which had been rough and boisterous in the early part of the month, now softened to gentler winds and light, misty rains. Tokwit said the whales might be close in-shore, but none had been sighted recently from the village. Atlin wanted his first hunt to be a real one and said they should go out to the main whaling grounds.

"You are the Chief," Tokwit said at once. "We shall find the whales where you say."

The ready answer made Atlin feel foolish and he glanced quickly at his great uncle to see if he was joking. But Tokwit's face was calm and serious. "I did not mean that the whales will surely be there," said Atlin. "Only that I want to go well out to start hunting."

"You would not want it unless you felt they would be there," Tokwit's face was still serious. "That is important. I will tell Kon-gass. His canoe will follow yours and when you have planted the first harpoon you must call on him to thrust the second."

"Why?" asked Atlin. He had thought of himself killing alone, from the first thrust until the last.

"Because a great Chief is not jealous. He shares what is his and asks others to help him."

The New Whale Chief

Atlin was not willing to give up his dream so easily. "But if I do not need help?"

"There will be a time when you do. Then, if others are used to helping you they will be quick and ready."

The two canoes put out together into the grey dusk of late evening. Soon they were paddling in darkness through the misty rain. It was cold and the sea heaved smoothly and ponderously, but the canoes slid easily over the swells and came to the hunting grounds long before dawn. Huddled alone in the bow, Atlin wondered about himself. The great shaft of his harpoon was beside him; the head was secured, the blade so sharp that it would split a hair drawn across it. He felt the sinewy strength of the lanyard and the light threads that held it to the shaft. Behind him, he knew, the coils of line were ready and the four floats were inflated. The crew was his Father's; every man there had taken part in the killing of a score or more of whales. Some, like Shiyus, who was also the diver, and Wewiks, the fourth paddler, were old now, but they were men to trust and depend on. Only he himself was untried. He knew they believed in him, as he believed in himself. Yet he knew also that many things could go against a whaler, even a great whaler like Nit-gass. When things went against a whaler, people said it was because his power was not strong, because he had not bathed and prayed regularly, because his tumanos was not working for him. Yet if things went badly for a whaler and he killed the whale in spite of them, as Nit-gass had many times, people said his power must be very strong.

While he thought of all these things, Atlin was listening hard for the sound of whales moving in the darkness, the sort of sounds he had sometimes heard as he waited beside Nit-gass for the dawn to come. But he heard only the rustle of the canoe as it lifted to the swells and the movement of the rips somewhere in the misty darkness. Earlier there had been the soft singing of the paddlers behind him, but now even that was silent. He wanted very much to hear the whales, to be sure they were there. If he struck one and the harpoon pulled loose or the whale ran far out to sea, he would at least be sure he had the beginnings of power. But if there were no whales he could be sure of nothing.

He moved a little, huddling closer into the warmth of his bear robe, and felt the touch of Hagilt's hand on his arm. "You are awake, Chief. A whaler should learn to sleep before he hunts. Then his arms and his eyes will be strong."

"There is much to think of," Atlin said.

"It is not the time to think. There is plenty of time to think in the nights when you are bathing alone or when you go to speak with your tumanos."

"The whale is not thinking," said Shiyus. "He has thought already and knows what he will do."

"Then I hope he has thought well of my harpoon," said Atlin. "To take it to his heart."

Shiyus laughed. "You know the words, Chief. If the whale knows them too you will have no trouble. Now sleep." He began to sing, very softly, the good weather songs of the Hotsath people. Huddled in the bear robe, Atlin smiled at the soothing words he had heard so often. He began to think of the people who had sung them and the places where he had heard them. In a little while he was asleep.

When he woke the dawn light had just begun to filter into the misty rain. The others were already awake and moving and Shiyus laughed at him. "You are lucky the whale didn't come and steal your harpoon, Chief. He could have run off with it and not wakened you."

"That is how a chief should sleep," said Hagilt. "Now he will be quick and strong."

Atlin's legs were cramped. He stood up and stretched, feeling the blood flow warmly through him. His eyes caught the flicker of a small bird's flight through the mist and behind him

The New Whale Chief

Tokwit said: "It is your day, Chief. Gakatas was watching for you through the night." A moment later they heard whales blowing. They were distant, but Atlin heard himself shout and Tokwit started the crew into the hunt.

The whales blew again, twice, within hearing, but they seemed to be travelling fast and were soon lost in the mist. The two canoes hunted steadily together through the morning, but found nothing else. Shortly after noon the wind freshened a little and the clouds and mist lifted, though the sky was still grey. Then, far to the south, Atlin saw the spouts of five whales. He swung his arm and both crews watched. The whales blew again, then again, on a line directly towards the canoes. "They are coming to you, Chief," Tokwit said quietly. "We can wait for them here."

The whales blew once again, then dived. Five minutes passed while the canoes watched and waited. Atlin looked back over the lines and floats and the ready paddlers. He bent down, picked up the great harpoon shaft and stood with it resting easily across his thighs. The thickness of the grip felt good in his hands, the weight and balance of the weapon seemed familiar and reassuring. His heart was beating fast, but he scarcely noticed it. Five minutes had become ten and the thought crossed his mind that the whales had turned under water and slipped away from them. Then a whale broke and spouted on the crest of a swell not a hundred feet away, headed directly towards the canoe. Tokwit shouted an order. The canoe swung sharply on to the line of the whale's travel and Atlin jumped to his place, his right foot firmly planted on the double bow thwart, his left on the right gunwale. He swung the harpoon across his chest, balancing easily to the heave and thrust of the swells, watching the water ahead and below. Then he saw the mottled grey back of the whale lifting through the grey water, a little to the right of the canoe's prow. He shouted and signalled with his harpoon. The whale seemed huge and unbelievably swift, but the canoe picked up speed and was only a little behind when the hoary head heaved out and the spout burst in a sharp explosion of moisture-saturated air. Atlin heard other spouts nearby, but his eyes were only for the whale that was his.

Standing to his steering paddle in the stern, watchful and wise, Tokwit knew it was not a good chance for a young harpooneer. The whale was travelling too fast, the freshening breeze broke the smooth rhythm of the swells and made it difficult to run in close. But they were committed. There was nothing he could do now but steer as close as he dared and let Atlin make his thrust. The whale's back had started down. He watched the swing of the tail flukes.

From his high place on the bow, Atlin also watched the whale draw down. Racing and pitching alongside the huge and dripping back, he had felt his body drawn up into the same elation he had felt on the night when he saw the shark at the Pool. Nothing was too great for his strength. His body was a spring, waiting for Tokwit's cry and the touch of Hagilt's paddle on his calf that would release its thrust.

The body of the whale had sunk down into the waves now. He swung the heavy harpoon shaft as he had seen Nit-gass do it and was ready. His eyes had chosen the point he would thrust for, high above the trailing edge of the short, rounded pectoral fin. Now he saw he was too far behind it and altogether too wide of the whale for a strong downward thrust. He shouted desperately: "Closer. Go closer." The bow of the canoe swung in a little, but only a little. Then he heard Tokwit's cry and knew he must make the thrust.

It was an awkward, reaching angle, more outward than downward, into the whale's side instead of his back. But he felt his blade cut smoothly into the blubber, with the full force of his body behind it. As the thrust spent itself the canoe wrenched away, Atlin tried to free his shaft, felt it loosen,

146

then found himself in the seething water, between the whale and the canoe, the shaft in his right hand. Everything about him was moving and he saw the heavy line drawing swiftly away. Then a great surge of water from the whale's driving tail flukes forced him towards the canoe. He felt the rasp of the line against his left leg; a moment later his free hand was grasping the gunwale of the canoe and Hagilt's shocked and anxious face was staring down at him. Atlin shook the water out of his hair and laughed. "Help me," he said and scrambled aboard, still grasping his shaft.

Lightly struck, already travelling fast, the whale was wild. He swam at the surface, thrashing with his tail, sending the spray flying all about him while the line hissed into the water. Soon all four floats were overboard and only the coil of light line was left. Hagilt took a wrap on a thwart and held the strain while the canoe raced through the sea. But the pace was too great, threatening to drag the canoe under, and he let it go. Atlin watched him in disappointment.

"It was a good thrust, Hawil," Hagilt said. "He will not pull loose."

"It will not kill him," answered Atlin.

"That is true, Hawil," said Tokwit. "But you shall cut his saddle. See, he has turned from the others already."

18. The First Whale

THE CHASE of Atlin's first whale was swift and strenuous. For an hour or more the whale fled at the surface or near it and the canoes tried to keep up with him. Then he sounded for fifteen or twenty minutes and the canoes circled, hoping to come up with him when he surfaced again. Atlin had forgotten that he wanted to kill alone and called to his uncle in the second canoe: "He is not struck deeply, Chief Kon-gass. Strike him to the heart for me and I will give you his tongue and his flippers."

"I saw it, Hawil. It was a good thrust. He has your harpoon and will not loose it. But I will strike him for you if I can."

The whale surfaced then, well away from both canoes, and ran again. He was slower now, but they still could not come up with him.

"Your whales are too fast, Chief," said Shiyus. "You must learn to swim more slowly when you bathe or you will wear us all out."

"The Chief is young," said Hagilt. "His whales are young and fast too."

"Then let him get a wife," said Shiyus, "and teach her to lie quietly under a blanket when he is hunting."

The crew laughed at this but the fourth paddler, who was older than Shiyus or any other man aboard, said: "If the young

Chief always strikes as surely as he struck this time, you had better find his whales close to the shore."

"Why is that, old man?" asked Hagilt.

"Because they will spout blood from the thrust and roll over and die. Then you will be towing. It is better to tow than to chase?"

Hagilt laughed. "What you say is true. But this time we shall chase *and* tow unless the Chief can turn Ma-ak in towards the land."

The whale had sounded again and again the canoes circled in wait. He broke at last in an angry flurry, very near Kon-gass' canoe, then began to swim slowly towards the coastline. Atlin called again: "Strike him for me, Chief Kon-gass," and picked up his own harpoon as Tokwit urged the paddlers in pursuit.

Kon-gass' canoe closed quickly and easily with the whale. Atlin watched anxiously. His uncle stood and swung his harpoon shaft as the whale's head plowed down, into the back of a swell. The canoe rode smoothly, very close. The thrust was strong and deep, straight down. The whale responded instantly in a burst of speed that hid everything in flying spray and drove him half out of the water in a rolling movement that showed the grooves of his throat and chest. He spouted blood and drew down again.

"Ugh," said Hagilt. "That was a mighty stroke. It will kill him very quickly."

"You have great power, Hawil," said Shiyus. "Chief Kon-gass has never made such a stroke before."

They passed Kon-gass' canoe and saw that all was well, though it was full of water and rolling sluggishly as the bailers worked. Atlin knew that four more floats were ready behind him on the short second line and stood again on the thwart with his harpoon ready.

"Strike quickly, Hawil," said Tokwit. "He is dying already and may sink. We must have more floats on him."

Atlin understood. When they closed he darted the harpoon rather than thrust it, letting the shaft slide through his hands and set the head on the whale's back with little more force than its own weight. The whale scarcely moved from the thrust. He was rolling awkwardly now, beginning to circle. There was blood in his spout, blood in the water along his sides and behind him. Hagilt had picked up the first line and the men were bending more floats to it. Atlin turned for the killing lance, but Tokwit shook his head. "Not yet, Hawil. If he does not die quickly, yes. But there is no need to make him angry and risk breaking the canoe."

Kon-gass' canoe had come up with them and now bent four more floats to the second line. They watched the whale flounder slowly through the water, dragging the floats behind him. He had turned out to sea again now and Hagilt began a slow, soothing song that was taken up by the other men:

"Go home," they sang
"Go straight home to the village of our people
"Turn your other flipper, whale,
"Paddle towards our home
"Paddle home to the village of our people."

They paddled as they sang, slowly, in time to the song, and Tokwit swung the canoe until it was on a course to meet the whale. Shiyus handed Atlin the killing lance.

"Perhaps he will turn for you, Hawil," said Tokwit. "It is well to try before you kill him."

With dreamlike slowness, canoe and whale came together. Tokwit held the canoe on a course just to the left of the whale's head and level with it. The paddlers sang steadily. Atlin could see the whale's mouth opening and closing to show the yellow-fringed baleen plates; he saw the little eye set back behind the hinge of the jaw and thought it saw him. He, too, was singing and now he pressed the point of the killing lance against the side of the whale's head. The whale turned more sharply and increased his speed a little. Atlin stopped singing and spoke to him: "You have my good harpoon, Ma-ak, my first harpoon. It is what you wanted. Swim with it now to the village of my people who are waiting to welcome you."

The whale was heading directly towards shore again and Tokwit let the canoe drop behind him. Both canoes followed at a little distance.

"He understands what you have told him, Hawil," said Tokwit. "Truly you have great power. But if he turns out again, you had better kill him."

The whale was rolling as he swam and two of the lines were wrapped around his body, so that the floats were drawn up very close to him. It seemed to Atlin that there was less blood in his spout each time and he began to feel anxious again. There were many stories of gravely wounded whales which had suddenly recovered and escaped.

"Should we put more drag on him?" he asked Tokwit. "Make him tow the line baskets or the canoes?"

Tokwit shook his head: "He is swimming well for you, Hawil. If you change anything he may turn away again."

From his slow swimming, the whale lunged suddenly forward, his body half out of the water. He fell back, instantly flipped over and sounded. The floats bobbed and raced and finally drew together in a straining cluster, but they were not dragged under. They moved on in a slow, troubled way towards the distant shore. The canoes closed in until Atlin could see the blood and bubbles trailing up through the grey-green water. He stood ready with the killing harpoon, for he knew that Ma-ak's dying strength had many times been known to turn against the canoes and break them. He could see the tangled lines straining almost straight down, dragging the untidy cluster of half-submerged floats. For a moment he thought he could see, deep down, the twisting flash of a great, shadowy body. Then the floats began to move more quickly, bobbing and slapping against one another. Less than two hundred feet away the whale came straight out of the water, heaving higher and higher until only the tail flukes were still hidden. For a moment it seemed suspended against the sky, then the heavy body shuddered and fell back with a mighty splash. Thick, black blood spouted unevenly from the blow-hole, staining the foamy water. The whale rolled over once more and died.

There was no doubt he was dead and the canoes closed at once, bending on more floats, shortening lines to bring the others closer. The whale was floating with its belly almost awash, its head far down. Shiyus, who was usually the diver, looked down with distaste through the bloodstained water at the long jaws half-open. He picked up a coil of strong line and felt for the knife that hung by a cord from his neck. "It is very deep," he said gloomily.

"Give me the rope, Shiyus," said Atlin eagerly. "I am a good diver."

"I know that, Hawil," said Shiyus slowly. "But do you know how to do it?"

"I have watched you many times," said Atlin. "Give me the rope and let me go." He had forgotten he was a chief and remembered only that he wanted to do this new thing.

Shiyus laughed and handed him the coil. "You were not afraid to dive for him when he was alive, Hawil. He should close his mouth more easily for you than he would for me."

Atlin slipped overboard, looked down and dived. It was deeper than he thought and harder to force himself down through the water than he had expected. But at last his hand touched, then gripped the lower jaw. He felt for the bones, drove his knife through the soft flesh between them, passed one end of the rope through and quickly knotted it. He reached for the upper jaw, but his ears were hurting and his head and chest were ready to burst, so he let go and shot back to the surface, still holding the rope. He drew a great breath of air and saw Shiyus peering anxiously at him. He held up the loop of rope in his hand.

"You have tied it already?" said Shiyus. "Good. In the upper jaw you must find the lip. It is strong, but cut close to the bone."

Atlin nodded and dived again. With the rope to help him, it was easy to get down this time. He found the upper jaw and the tough rubbery lip beyond the baleen plates. It was hard to force the shell knife through, but he managed it and lengthened the cut along the bone until the rope passed easily through it. Then he surfaced again, passed the rope to Shiyus and climbed back into the canoe.

Shiyus and Hagilt heaved on the rope. Staring down into the water, Atlin watched the lower jaw pull slowly shut as the rope dragged through the cut in the upper lip. Then the head lifted until it was only five or six feet under water. Hagilt held the strain while Shiyus bent on two floats. They were ready to tow.

Both canoes had lines on the whale, passing under their keels to the right side of the forward thwart. A short line from the left side of the after thwart was tied again to the tow line to keep the pull straight. The light was fading and the misty rain had closed in on them again, but the light southerly breeze held and Tokwit steered by it. The men sang steadily, keeping the slow rhythms with their paddles. It seemed to Atlin they scarcely moved against the water. Behind them the whale's body heaved and sloshed in the swells, the shining wet floats dancing around it. Atlin was very tired and his body ached, but he sang with the others and dipped his paddle in steady strokes. It grew dark and behind him Hagilt said: "Rest, Hawil. It is not for a Chief to tow his whale."

"I am not tired," said Atlin.

"Rest," said Hagilt. "You will be a great chief, but you must learn to rest and to think."

"What Hagilt says is true," said Shiyus. "A chief must think. He must have strength when others have not. Rest now and guard your strength."

Atlin put down his paddle, pulled his robe about his shoulders and settled back against the thwart. Nothing had been as he had expected it. Yet he had struck the whale, his line had held fast and the whale was dead. By all the laws, he knew, it was his whale. The triumph was his, the saddle of the whale was his, the fin tip that all whalers kept as a record of their kills was his. Yet Kon-gass had killed it.

As though he knew Atlin's thoughts, Hagilt said. "You have done well, Hawil. It is not often a young chief brings in a whale from his first hunt."

"I did not kill the whale," answered Atlin. "Chief Kon-gass killed him."

"It was a good thrust," agreed Hagilt. "It was the death thrust. But the whale was already yours. It will be said that your tumanos guided Kon-gass' thrust."

"Chief Kon-gass guided the thrust," said Atlin. "It was the thrust of a strong man. Perhaps I am not yet strong enough to make such a thrust."

"You could have made it just as strongly."

Atlin laughed. "Next time I will show you. But this time I shall give Kon-gass the tongue and the flippers as I promised ... and the fin tip as well."

Hagilt was silent for some while. Then he answered: "I have not heard of such a thing. It is a great chief's thought. Only the son of Nit-gass would have found it."

19. Chief Eskowit's Daughter

DURING HIS first season, Atlin killed three more whales. He struck several others, but they escaped in various ways—sometimes the harpoon head was not well set and pulled out, once a line broke, once a bad storm came up and they had to cut loose. To Atlin it seemed a season of mistakes and missed opportunities, in spite of his triumphs, but Tokwit told him he was wrong.

"All whalers make mistakes. Even Nit-gass did Whales are more powerful than men. A young whaler must learn by making mistakes. He must learn you cannot tell what a whale will do. That is how he grows in power and his mistakes become fewer."

"Yet if a man had really great power the whales would do as he wished."

"No," said Tokwit. "A whale is always stronger than a man. A man must learn his ways and follow them. A great whaler must learn to think as a whale thinks, then he can use the whale's strength to bring him to the beach."

Atlin thought for a few moments, then he said: "These are true things. Yet when we close with a whale and I am standing on the bow with my harpoon in my hands, I feel I have the strength of a hundred whales."

Tokwit laughed. "Nit-gass thought the same thing. That is why you are bold and why you strike well. But it is not enough. Why is it that you wear the head-band of red cedar bark and the hemlock branch?"

"Those are for humility."

"Very well," said Tokwit. "Remember them. Remember that not all of a man's strength is in his hands and his heart. He must also learn and understand."

Tetacus told Atlin much the same things, then he added: "It is time for you to take a wife. We spoke about it before. Have you thought of it?"

"Yes, grandfather," said Atlin.

"I spoke to you then of Chief Eskowit's daughters. But there are other great chiefs who have daughters."

"I have thought of it many times, Hawil," said Atlin. "And in my thoughts I find always Watsika, the daughter of Eskowit. I do not know why."

Tetacus smiled. "She is tall and very beautiful, with light skin and light hair. Her ankles and wrists are slim and her voice sings. Perhaps that is why. She is Eskowit's second daughter, but his favourite."

"I have seen her only once," said Atlin. "But she is the one I remember."

"Very well," said Tetacus. "We will send Tokwit to speak for you."

Tokwit left a few days later with three other leading men of the tribe, taking a magnificent sea otter robe as a proposal gift to Chief Eskowit. It was Tokwit's duty to speak of the virtues and advantages of the marriage and to leave the gift, which would be returned if the proposal were not accepted.

Tokwit came back and reported that Chief Eskowit had listened carefully, but had said nothing, which was expected. Then, a few days later, a Tsitikat canoe came to return the sea otter robe, which meant that the proposal was rejected.

"It is nothing," Tetacus said. "A great chief always returns the gift once, perhaps many times, unless it has been arranged otherwise. In a few days Tokwit will take it back to him again."

But Atlin felt his old anger against Eskowit. "He does not want me," he said. "He had no love for my Father and he has no reason to love me."

Tetacus turned to Tokwit. "Are there other suitors?"

"Yes," answered Tokwit, "but they are sons of lesser chiefs than Nit-gass."

Tetacus turned on his heel and paced slowly back and forth, considering the matter. "It is a good match," he said at last. "If there has been bad feeling between our houses it is the more reason to heal it by marriage. Go again, Tokwit, and urge these things upon the Chief. Tell him that the sons of Atlin and Watsika will inherit all the honours and privileges of our house. He knows they are many."

So Tokwit went again, and again the gift was returned. This time Tetacus became angry. "Does he think we are slaves or commoners, to be treated in such a way? How often does he think we will go back to him?"

"I do not know, Hawil," said Tokwit respectfully. "But I have heard that the gifts of all the other suitors have been returned."

Tetacus, who had bent his head in thought, looked up sharply. "Ah! Then he wants something more from us. But what is it?"

Atlin laughed angrily. "Perhaps he wants the sea lion he stole from me, Hawil."

Tetacus frowned. "It is not good to say such things, even as a joke. The law was obeyed."

"Chief Eskowit is a jealous man, Hawil," said Tokwit. "He does not forget easily. Perhaps the Young Chief is right."

Atlin understood then that the matter was a serious one.

Whenever important decisions were to be made the older men called him the Young Chief. When the decisions were about lesser matters in which he could take full part they called him "Chief" or "Hawil".

Tetacus shook his head solemnly at Tokwit's words. "The Young Chief has seen the daughter of Eskowit and felt her beauty. Once that has happened, no young man's judgment is wise."

"Chief Eskowit is a young man also," answered Tokwit. "Not in years, but in wisdom. That is why the Young Chief may be right."

"Very well," said Tetacus, plainly unconvinced. "I will go myself and talk with Chief Eskowit."

"Let me go, Hawil," said Atlin. "I will wait outside the door of the Chief's long house until they ask me to come in."

"And if they do not ask you?" said Tokwit. "That is an ordinary man's way of asking for a wife, not the way of a Great Chief. Eskowit would make a joke of you."

"No," said Tetacus. "Neither you nor I will go begging. Instead, we will wait. I will let it be known that the Young Chief still wishes to marry Watsika, but we are no longer sure this is wise. Chief Eskowit will quickly hear of it. Very soon now we shall be going to the winter dance of the Kashutl people. It will make much talk and we shall hear what Eskowit is thinking."

Atlin felt his heart sink. Though the idea of marriage had at first seemed strange and distant to him, almost a joke, and though he had seen Watsika only once, he now felt a great tenderness for her. "But, Hawil," he protested. "Chief Eskowit may give Watsika to one of the others."

"He may think with the jealous heart of a child," said Tetacus, "but he will not give her to the son of a small chief when a great chief's son is waiting. I will let it be known that you are young and in no hurry. He knows that the chiefs of the

Moachats, the Kuyuquots and the Ohotisats all have un-
married daughters. We shall soon learn his thoughts."

And so the matter was left, to Atlin's strong dissatisfaction.
But he knew that the wife of Hagilt was a cousin of Chief
Eskowit, so he told Hagilt his fears. Hagilt laughed heartily.
"So you have eyes for more than whales, Chief," he said.
"That is good. Have you spoken to her?"

"No," said Atlin. "How can it be done?"

"Perhaps it would be better not to try. Soon we shall go to
visit my wife's cousins. My wife is very wise in such things.
She would take a message for you to Watsika."

"Will that help?"

Hagilt laughed again. "Does whale oil brighten the fire?
Does thunder shake the mountains? The wishes of a man's
favourite daughter are stronger than any of these things."

20. *The Mind of Eskowit*

As TETACUS had expected, the explanation of Chief Eskowit's reluctance came from the gossip of the Kashutl winter dance. Tokwit collected it carefully from many sources and put it all together at a meeting of the Hotsath chiefs.

"It is as the Young Chief thought," he said "Eskowit has not forgotten the sea lion. He believes he was shamed and made small before his people. Now, if he gives his daughter to the man who shamed him, he will seem nothing at all."

"It is a small man that thinks so," said Tetacus. "Any other would know that by giving his daughter freely he would seem big, not small."

"Yet that is his thought," said Tokwit, "and it is deeply in his heart. Even Watsika has not been able to change him, though the people say she has tried."

"If that is so," said Tetacus. "Why does he not give her to one of the other suitors?"

"They say it is not easy for him," answered Tokwit. "It is well known that the Chief's wife is a woman of great strength. It is known, too, that many of the Tsitikat chiefs think Eskowit is wrong. In his heart, he himself knows he is wrong and because he is a weak man he will do nothing."

"It is true he is weak," said Tetacus. "But it is hardest to change a weak man when he is wrong. We must think his thoughts and try to find a way for him to change."

Atlin listened and said nothing. Little that was said was new to him. He knew that his mother, Aneetsa, had sent a message to Chief Eskowit's wife, who, like herself, was the daughter of a Kashutl chief. And Hagilt had brought him word that Watsika favoured him and would try to win her father over. He had thought of many possibilities and dreamed many dreams in the weeks that had passed: he would take Watsika in war, he would meet her secretly and steal her away, he would go himself and demand her from Eskowit with bold and angry words. But none of these things was real to him, because they were against his training and the ways of his people. He listened in silence to the words of the older men because he knew they understood the ways of ceremony and privilege that governed the marriages of the sons and daughters of great chiefs.

Even though he was convinced he loved Watsika, she did not fill Atlin's thoughts. It was a mild and gentle winter, with few long periods of stormy weather. The seal hunters and halibut fishermen were able to get out a great deal and brought in good catches; with these and the whales that Atlin and Kon-gass had brought in during the previous summer, the Hotsath people wintered well. Atlin himself, with Hinak, frequently went out after seals and porpoises and several times on these expeditions they saw humpback whales and killer whales. Once a killer whale surfaced so close to the canoe that Atlin leapt instantly to thwart and gunwale and drove his seal spear as though it were a harpoon. The thrust shattered the shaft, but drove both points securely home. The whale ran instantly, the light line held and the tiny canoe raced through the water. Atlin threw his weight over to balance the canoe, watched the straining line, listened to the hiss of water against the sharp prow and shouted with joy. In the stern

Hinak steered as best he could and wondered whether he should try to blow up the sealskin float that was lying at his feet. He picked it up and fumbled for the mouthpiece, holding his paddle in one hand.

Atlin glanced round and shook his head. "We can't hold him," he said. "Something will give."

Just then the whale surfaced, blew lazily, and sounded with sudden violence. The canoe heeled dangerously to the right. Atlin flung his body overboard on the left, holding on with one hand and reaching for his knife with the other. The light line broke, the canoe bounced half out of the water and almost capsized before Atlin and Hinak could shift their weight again to balance it.

This was a hunter's joke, good to remember and good to talk about. But it gave Atlin an idea for using the good winter weather. He asked Tokwit if the crews would go out with the big canoes. Tokwit smiled. "No," he said. "They want to stay with their wives beside the fires and eat too much and drink too much. It is sport for young men. The Sorefaces are few and it is hard to come near the killer whales because they are fast and wary. Besides, it is cold out there and likely to blow up a storm at any time."

"Will you come if I get a crew of young men?"

"No," said Tokwit again. "It is enough to go with you in the summer. Take a young man like Witamis for your steersman. He will learn a lot. The killer whales have little oil and you will work hard for that, but they are good for training young whalers."

No one had hunted killer whales since Nit-gass was a young man, but Atlin had no difficulty in collecting a crew of boys and young men. They put out to hunt in the first spell of calm weather, hoping to find a solitary humpback close inshore. On the first day they saw neither humpbacks nor killers. On the second day they found a small school of killer whales near

Seal Rocks, just below Shark Island. The whales were circling lazily, perhaps hunting for seals, when they first saw them and Atlin approached directly, expecting to close easily. When the canoe was within two or three hundred feet the whales blew and sounded one by one, seemingly unconcerned. But when they showed again they were half a mile to seaward, closely schooled and travelling south.

"We could chase them, Hawil," said Witamis hopefully. "They will not go fast for long."

But even Atlin's slight experience had taught him that the swiftest canoe cannot catch up to an escaping whale. "No," he said, "it is better to look for others."

A few days later, after a heavy storm, they surprised an old humpback male lying at the surface with one huge flipper waving in the air. The chase was too eager. Some sound from the canoe reached the old whale. He righted himself and began swimming. Through the rest of the day he played with them, rarely sounding for longer than four or five minutes, coming up always where he was least expected, tempting them on and on until at dusk they wearily turned and left him. Tokwit laughed when Atlin told him of it. "To kill an old one like that you must catch him sleeping. And when you do, you had better strike deep and go away from him fast. The old ones have bad tempers."

On the next hunt they found another small school of killers Atlin warned his crew to paddle calmly and quietly and told Witamis to steer well to one side of the school. They were very close when the whales dived and Atlin took his place on the bow thwart, though he had little real hope that anything would come of it. Then he saw the bulge of water from a whale's moving body directly ahead of the canoe. He pointed and shouted to his crew. A small female rolled up and blew and they caught up with her easily. Witamis shouted from the stern and Atlin made his thrust, feeling the harpoon head drive true and deep. He dropped instantly down into the bow space and felt the canoe shiver and lurch mightily as he did so. He jumped to his feet again and met a deluge of angry water thrown up by the tail flukes. The fourth paddler jumped overboard in panic. The first coil of line and the first float swept out freely, but a kink in the second coil caught briefly in the thwart, wrenched it loose and stunned Hinak in the first paddler's place. As Atlin reached over to lift him out of the water that now filled the canoe to the gunwales, the last coil of line and the last two floats disappeared safely overboard.

Atlin grimly took stock. The canoe sloshed and wallowed uncomfortably in the easy swell, its right gunwale split from end to end by the fierce blow of the whale's tail flukes. Witamis sat open-mouthed in the stern. Hinak was recovering. The third paddler was helping the fourth back aboard.

"Bail," said Atlin sharply. "Get the water out."

"Where is the whale?" asked Witamis.

"We will find her," said Atlin. "She is deeply struck. But first get the water out." He felt Hinak's head where the thwart had struck it. "Are you all right, my brother?"

"Did the whale hit me?" asked Hinak, still dazed.

"No," said Atlin, laughing. "The canoe." He felt strong and sure when he saw the confusion of the others and the feeling pleased him. "It is lucky the whale was only a little one," he said.

"What was wrong?" asked Witamis, bailing steadily.

"You did not wait for the tail flukes to swing out," said Atlin. "And the fourth and sixth paddlers did not backwater fast enough, or else you were too close. But that is good."

"The people will laugh at us when they see the canoe," said Witamis gloomily.

"But we shall have the whale," said Atlin, pointing to seaward where the wounded whale was circling feebly, dragging the floats behind her. "We can laugh a little too."

The Mind of Eskowit

When they had cleared the canoe of water and came up with the whale, she was on her side, showing the brilliant white of her belly, barely moving. As the canoe drew close she made a feeble effort to dive, came up almost instantly and spouted blood. Atlin hesitated a moment, then picked up the killing lance. "Go in from the side," he ordered. "Near the flipper Give me time to strike twice, then back water on both sides."

It was a cautious, even timid approach, for the crew had a new respect for whales, even small ones. Atlin edged his left foot far forward on the broken gunwale, raised the lance and thrust twice, swiftly and deeply, in the way of Nit-gass. A shudder ran through the whale's body as the canoe backed off; her tail flukes swirled heavily, her head and fore-body half lifted from the water and fell back. Atlin watched, letting the bloody lance point trail in the water. "Let them laugh," he said. "When they cut out my harpoon they will find she took it to her heart."

Atlin hunted with his young whalers through the winter, whenever the weather was calm. They made few kills but, as Tokwit had promised, they learned steadily. Long before the end of the winter it was clear that Hinak, who paddled strongly and steadily, would be able to replace Shiyus in the regular crew, while Witamis could replace the fourth paddler, whose knees and shoulders hurt him.

Atlin was already bathing regularly, through every waxing moon, in preparation for the coming season. Alone at the Forks, on the beaches or on the rocks of Round Hill Point, he thought often of Watsika and of Eskowit. Whenever he did so he found himself remembering the words of Tetacus: "We must think his thoughts and try to find a way for him to change." It was not easy to think Eskowit's thoughts. Yet one thing came back again and again to Atlin's mind: Eskowit had wanted to claim Nit-gass' power. More than that; he had lied about it and claimed that he had it through the finding of

Nit-gass' body on his beaches. His claim had been answered and even made ridiculous by the affair of the sea lion.

Less clearly, Atlin realised that Eskowit needed power and the appearance of power. He himself needed power to give his crew confidence in him, needed the feel of it to go in boldly against a whale and thrust deeply and surely at the right moment. But much of his power was in himself, even without the help of the spirits; it was in the quickness of his eyes to see the whales, in judging which way they would go, in the strength of his arms and shoulders that made the thrust, in the quickness and rightness of whatever orders he had to give after the whale was harpooned. Eskowit could only send out his power and hope that it would bring dead whales to his beaches. If for any reason it was not strong enough, he could not help it with his hands or his quickness or his boldness.

Thinking these things, Atlin felt sometimes that the answer to his difficulties was very close. Bathing with Hinak from the rocks of Round Hill Point during the herring spawn moon, he spoke of it: "Do you believe that Eskowit has power?"

Hinak shivered in the moonlight. "Yes. He can make very strong magic. All the chiefs who bring dead whales to the beaches must make strong magic."

"Nit-gass, my father, said that the currents set well to bring dead things to his beaches and we know that is true."

"Even so, he has great power. No man who had not would dare to bathe with a corpse tied to his back or even to go to the burial island and take a corpse from its place."

Atlin laughed. When he heard such things, the voice of Nit-gass was always close to him, ready to laugh also. "If he has such power, how could we take it from him when we freed the sea lion? Why did he not make the sea lion die and drift to his beaches?"

"I don't know," said Hinak. "Unless your kind of power is greater than his."

166

Atlin laughed again. "Yet when I want to give him back whatever I have taken from him, I do not know how to. So, in the end, my power is weak also."

"No," said Hinak. "It is a different kind of power. There is a way for you to give him back what you took, and he will not be able to refuse it."

21. *Three Whales*

THE FIRST whale of the new season was one of a small school of humpbacks that came in close to shore and was seen from the village. The canoes put out at once and Tokwit steered to a skilful interception. The whales were travelling north, so Atlin selected the one on the seaward flank and they closed with it quickly and easily. The sea was quiet and Atlin's thrust was accurate and powerful, almost straight down and directly behind the flipper. He uttered a shout of satisfaction as he felt the blade drive down and shatter deep in the whale, recovered smoothly and twisted the shaft free. In the same movement, he dropped down into the bow space and turned to watch the line run out through the spray and confusion of the whale's flight. From the stern Tokwit saluted him with a hand lifted from his paddle.

The rest of the school sounded, but the wounded whale turned instantly seaward in its panic. The canoe swung and the lines leapt smoothly out from their coils. As the last float went over, Atlin turned from watching it to see the whale jump right out of the water and fall back with a heavy splash. Even after it had fallen back, he could still see in his mind the thick, powerful body suspended in the clear air over the gently heaving sea, the heavy line trailing from the deep wound in its back. It was a moment of elation and a memory that would stay with him until he died—the memory of the first time his heart and mind and body, the crew behind him and the gear they used had worked perfectly together to achieve their purpose.

Tokwit had given his sharp command and the crew had already taken up the chase. The fourth paddler was blowing up more floats. Atlin called to Kon-gass to close with the whale and strike again as soon as he could. A dozen or more canoes that had put out from the village with them were scattered over the water and he could hear their people singing, urging the whale to swim slowly, to turn towards the village. Atlin opened his box, took out a spare lanyard and harpoon head and began fitting them carefully to his shaft. He grinned at Hinak who was paddling steadily behind him.

"This is better than chasing killer whales, eh?"

Hagilt grunted. "If the killer whales taught you to strike like that, Hawil, you should thank them, not laugh at them."

"We never closed so easily with a killer whale," said Hinak.

"That is true," said Hagilt. "They are quick and scare easily. But the others can be wild too. The Chief must have paid good attention to his bathing lately."

Both canoes were close to the whale now, which was travelling slowly at the surface, rolling awkwardly to its right side so that the long left flipper kept showing above the water. Atlin watched as Kon-gass' canoe closed in. Something in the way the whale was moving made him uneasy. He stood up and shouted: "Not now, Chief Kon-gass. Not now. Back off and wait."

It seemed as though his anxious voice had stirred the whale. her tail flukes churned the water violently, lunging her body forward, still half on its side. She curved over, went under, came out again and went on through a series of five massive lunges that threw blood and spray in a path behind her. Then she stopped again and rolled, seemingly exhausted, on the surface. Kon-gass' canoe, half-filled with water from the flurry, laboured in pursuit. Atlin's canoe drew alongside and Atlin glanced anxiously at his uncle, trying to judge whether he was offended. Kon-gass, whose handsome face nearly always had a worried look, turned from the whale. "What made you call to us, Nephew?" he asked. "A moment later and I would have struck."

"Something told me to call," answered Atlin. "I do not know what it was."

"It was your tumanos, and it saved us. Now the whale is dying." Kon-gass pointed to the thick black blood of the spout.

"True," said Atlin, "but there should be more floats or she may sink. Yours are ready. Will you bend some on for me, Chief?"

The whale died soon after, without another thrust, and a dozen canoes helped tow it in triumph to the beach. When it was on the beach and the butchering had begun Atlin told Hinak: "It could not be this one. Yet it should have been the first."

"It does not matter," Hinak answered. "A Chief's duty is to his own people first, even when he wants to get married. There is plenty of time. It can be the third whale or the tenth."

Atlin laughed. "They do not all die so easily. He may wait a long time."

When they next went out Atlin told Tokwit he wanted to hunt to the north, near the Halibut Bank and Hotsath Island. "It is a good place to find whales," said Tokwit. "But a bad place to kill them. You know how the currents set into Chief Eskowit's waters."

"I know it well," said Atlin. "Yet I want to hunt there."

The grey whales were passing through in good numbers, but they hunted for several days off Hotsath Island before they were able to come up with one and strike it. Though it was travelling north when Atlin set the harpoon it swung in a great circle and ran hard towards the south. The canoes had difficulty keeping whale or floats in sight until they came up with it off Round Hill Point and were able to strike again and bend on more floats. From there it ran again and towed Atlin's canoe until it died at nightfall, well out off the mouth of Kashutl Inlet.

As they began to tow in, helped by the currents, Tokwit said: "Your tumanos is working well for you, Hawil. He knew your home and brought you to it."

Atlin glanced at Hinak and smiled. Later, as they were towing in towards the beach, Hinak asked Atlin: "Why do you not tell them what you want?"

"It would not do," said Atlin. "If anything went against me they would say it was Eskowit's power and would not want to go there again."

As it was, Tokwit was easily persuaded the next time and the first whale they struck turned almost instantly south again. A heavy swell was running and Atlin's thrust, mistimed, had not gone deeply. After running for about a mile at the surface, the whale sounded, throwing his flukes high in the air, and the canoes lost him. They separated to search and ten or fifteen minutes later Atlin saw the spout, far to the south, then the lift of the tail as the whale sounded again. Kon-gass, searching well to seaward, had seen nothing, but Tokwit drove his paddlers to the chase.

They closed again, still north of Round Hill Point, and Atlin drove a second harpoon with two floats. The thrust was deeper this time, and better placed, but not mortal. The whale ran from it and sounded almost immediately, but the floats slowed him, dragging together and bouncing on the surface.

"He is still strong," Atlin told Tokwit. "We shall need more floats." He turned away, set a new head on his harpoon and began tying the lanyard to the shaft. Then Hinak shouted.

The whale had surfaced again and spouted. He had turned in his dive and was less than a hundred feet from the canoe. His head and back drew down and Atlin knew he was heading directly for the canoe. There was no time to reach for the killing lance. He sprang to the gunwale as Tokwit and the paddlers worked to swing the canoe bow on to the whale's rush. He saw the shadowy body of the whale through the swells, coming very fast, directly towards the left side of the bow. Every muscle in his body tensed and his eyes strained to recognise the shape of the whale's head and find his blowhole. In the last moment he saw it and drove the harpoon directly towards it. He felt a violent shock that tore the shaft from his hands, felt the jarring thud of the whale's head against the canoe, then found himself swimming in the heaving water. He shook the water out of his eyes and saw the canoe wallowing nearby, the crew clustered around it. Beyond it, in a threshing fury of blood and white water, the whale went into his death flurry.

Atlin swam to the canoe and found Tokwit hanging on to the stern with the fifth and sixth paddlers. The third and fourth paddlers were holding on to newly inflated floats. Hagilt and Hinak were near the bow. But the whole left side was split cleanly out of the canoe.

Tokwit said calmly: "You struck him well, Hawil. But he had better die quickly and not come back or it will be the end of us."

Atlin pulled himself up to look into the broken canoe. "There are still ropes and floats there," he said. "Even the line baskets. We can tie it together."

Tokwit nodded. "Yes," he agreed. "But give an old man a few moments to think. Kon-gass will soon be here."

Kon-gass found them about ten minutes later, when Tokwit

had already set his shivering crew to blowing up more floats
and Atlin, with Hagilt, was trying to fit the broken side of the
canoe back into place. With the second canoe alongside it was
fairly simple to lash the broken section in place, bail out the
water and caulk the leaks. Most of the gear was floating nearby
and the whale was already dead. As soon as he realised that
everyone was safe, Kon-gass' habitual worried look left him and
he became very cheerful.

"You will have to give old Solmic half the whale, Nephew,"
he told Atlin. "He doesn't like it when young Chiefs break
canoes."

"We will put in a word for you, Hawil," said Hagilt.
"Ma-ak was in an ugly mood today. If you hadn't made that
thrust he would have done us harm."

The crews laughed and joked in the release of tension as
they secured the whale for towing. Atlin, still jarred and
shaken by the impact of the whale's charge, did not join in.
His canoe and his best harpoon shaft were broken and again
the whale had run south. He began to wonder if it could be
that some power of Eskowit was working against him. Tokwit
noticed his concern and put a hand on his shoulder. "It was
well done, Hawil," he said. "A broken canoe is nothing.
Nit-gass broke many."

"I did not think a whale could turn so quickly," Atlin said.

"It was I who was slow," Tokwit answered. "I should have
known he would come back. But he is dead now and we are
alive. When he came for the canoe I did not think it would
be so."

Hagilt laughed at the last words. "You are too old to die,
Wise one," he said. "And the Chief is too young. We are well
guarded and should live a long while."

"Be sure you bathe properly and say your prayers, then,"
Tokwit told him. "You cannot expect the Chief to strike his
blade into the blowhole every time."

22. *Eskowit's Whale*

WHEN ATLIN told Tokwit he wanted to hunt again towards the north, the old steersman was not enthusiastic.

"It is a good place," Atlin said. "We find the whales there each time we go."

"True," agreed Tokwit. "But they will not always swim south for you."

"I do not want it," said Atlin.

Tokwit looked at him in surprise. "If they swim into Tsitikat waters Chief Eskowit will say you are stealing his whales. Even if you kill quickly there is danger of that because the currents run so strongly."

"That is what I want," said Atlin. "I want to kill a whale and take it to Chief Eskowit."

Tokwit turned slowly, leaning on his staff. "You would take it as a wedding gift for Watsika?"

"No," said Atlin, smiling at his great uncle's surprise. "I would take it to him in place of the sea lion, to show his power."

Tokwit stood gazing out over the sea for several seconds, then he nodded slowly. "It is a clever idea, Chief. There were so few storms last winter that only one whale drifted to the Tsitikat beaches. Eskowit cannot refuse the whale or his people would be angry." With his staff he drew the outline of a grey whale in the sand. "But he will not like you for it. It will make you a very great man, to give away a whale. I have not heard of it before."

"I shall not give it as though at a potlatch. I shall say that his power has brought it. He will be pleased."

Tokwit looked at his Chief in admiration. "Did Tetacus tell you this?"

"No," said Atlin. "Hinak and I spoke of it together. But he was the first to think of how it could be done."

"He has a wise head," Tokwit shook his own head and laughed with pleasure. "Together you have thought the thoughts of Eskowit and understood him. Because he is a small man he will pretend to himself that he believes you. The people will understand the truth. But to give away a whale and say you have not given it—that is a great thing that will be remembered to the end of time."

"I do not want to be remembered," said Atlin. "I want Watsika."

"Will you tell him so?"

Atlin recognised in Tokwit's voice the crafty tone he sometimes used when his questioning was a test. "No," he answered.

"Then what will you gain?"

"Perhaps nothing," answered Atlin. "But I think his heart wants to give what he has said he will not. When the whale is his he will be free to change his words."

The crews hunted northward for three days in the face of bright westerly winds, sighting only passing schools of grey whales with which they were unable to close. The fourth day was hazy, with a light breeze from the south. They had hunted over the Halibut Bank, almost to the north end of Hotsath Island, when Hagilt sighted the old bull humpback, close inshore. He was travelling northward, behind them, and had not seen them. He spouted twice more, then humped his dark back and sounded.

Both canoes raced in and turned northward again along the line he seemed to be following. Atlin looked back over the canoe that had been Nit-gass' favourite and saw that all the gear was in order. He turned to his harpoon with the untried shaft Hagilt had made for him, longer and heavier than any he had used till now. "For a young man," Hagilt had said. "You are very strong. Unless the shaft is as heavy as a man can use, much strength is wasted. When you grow stronger again I will make you another."

The whale surfaced midway between the two canoes and comfortably ahead of them. He was lazy, rolling comfortably along, suspecting nothing. Atlin picked up his harpoon and took his place as Tokwit closed in smoothly from the left. The whale blew again, drew down a little and they were alongside. Atlin saw only the shadowy flipper through the water ahead of the canoe and the place behind it where he meant to strike. He filled his lungs and swung the harpoon. Tokwit signalled, there was the confirming touch of Hagilt's paddle and Atlin drove his harpoon. He saw the blade enter, felt the thrust go down and down into the whale while everything else, whale and canoe and sea, seemed to stand still. He recovered as the thrust spent itself, withdrew the shaft and saw blood spurt. Then he dropped to the bow space as the whale humped his back and dived.

The heavy line ran out and the first float went over into water still swirling from the thrust of the whale's dive. There had been no splash, no deluge of water and the silence and swiftness with which everything had happened made Atlin vaguely uneasy. But Hagilt said: "You have killed him, Hawil. He has it in his heart."

"It went deep," Atlin said. "But I do not think he will die quickly."

All four floats were out now and Atlin watched anxiously for any sign that the whale might be turning. He had set a new point and lanyard on the harpoon shaft and now passed the loop of the lanyard back to Hagilt.

The whale surfaced suddenly in a wild jump that carried his thick body almost completely out of the water, fell back and spouted. He had turned slightly to seaward, but was travelling very slowly. "It is shallow here," said Tokwit. "I think he hit his head against the bottom."

"Will he turn?" asked Atlin anxiously.

"Who knows?" answered Tokwit. "But we can try to steer him."

Atlin picked up his harpoon and took his place. The two canoes were side by side, less than fifty feet apart. "Chief Kon-gass," Atlin said. "The Soreface is a gift for Chief Eskowit. I cannot give you any part of him. But if you will help me steer him to the north I will remember you when I strike again."

Kon-gass turned in surprise, then a broad smile changed his gentle, worried face. "I think I understand you, Hawil. We will help you."

Kon-gass' canoe closed with the whale, which was rolling awkwardly. Kon-gass struck from the side, placing his thrust well forward, but the whale held on his course.

"How much strength has he?" Atlin asked Tokwit.

"Too much," Tokwit said. "You have killed him. There was blood in his spout. But he will swim a long way before he dies."

"Then I will kill him here," said Atlin.

"Not yet," answered Tokwit. "Let Hagilt take the cutting lance and cut his tail flukes. He is still quiet from striking his head against the bottom."

Hinak handed Hagilt the short chisel-bladed lance from the thwart behind him and Hagilt stood with it, watching the whale closely as Tokwit took the canoe in. It was a part of whaling Atlin had never seen before, though he knew the purpose was to drive the sharp cutting lance at the base of the flukes and cut through the strong tendons that drove them. The whale was slow and awkward, blundering rather than swimming through the water. Tokwit brought the canoe close; Atlin and Hagilt watched the ponderous swing of the tail. It was deep in the water and Hagilt dropped to one knee, leaning out over the gunwale. Twice the flukes swung in towards the canoe, swirling the surface as they turned, but he did not strike. "It is too soon," he told Atlin. "He is swimming badly for us." But the flukes were closer to the surface on the next swing. Hagilt drove his lance, striking for the point where the leading edge of the left fluke joined the body. There was a split second of pause in which Atlin saw blood start from the wound, then a surge of water hit him in the face and chest as the whale sounded. The force of the water threw him dazed and gasping against the left side of the canoe. Hagilt was thrown against Hinak and for a moment the canoe heeled violently over. Then both crews began to laugh.

"You should have spoken to him, Hawil," said Hagilt ruefully, still gasping. "You should have told him to be quiet when I struck."

"Tokwit said he was stunned," said Atlin. "I did not think he would hear."

It was a good answer and everyone laughed again. "Did you cut him?" Tokwit asked.

"Yes," answered Hagilt.

"Then he will not be down long."

As Tokwit spoke, the whale surfaced again and spouted, showing blood. He had travelled northward in his dive and was now level with the north point of Hotsath Island. He had rolled in the lines and several of the floats were dragging and bouncing against his sides. His movements were erratic and uncertain. Hagilt had picked up the cutting lance again and moved over in front of Hinak. Tokwit tried several times to close from the right, but each time the whale sheered awkwardly and forced them away.

Atlin watched anxiously. He wanted to kill before they were seen from the Tsitikat village and the canoes put out. "It is time to kill him," he said.

"He is still strong," said Tokwit doubtfully. But he began to force the canoe up towards the whale's right flipper as Atlin picked up the killing lance. Again the uncertain movements of the whale, as well as the tangled lines and bouncing floats, kept them away. The whale was bleeding heavily from the working of the harpoon heads in his wounds. He was rolling a little, occasionally lifting his right flipper out of the water. As the canoe closed again Atlin ran forward along the gunwale, set one foot on the ears of the high prow and jumped to the whale's back.

He drove the lance instantly to the full length of the bone point and beyond, holding it there and trying to twist it as blood welled in the wound. The whale drew down almost smoothly; Atlin dropped to his knees and held on as the water closed over him. He felt no fear, only a determination to still the whale's huge bulk and make it his own. As the whale surfaced again Atlin drew out the lance and moved quickly to meet the whale's heavy roll to his left side. He drove the lance again, close above the flipper, felt the huge body shudder under his feet, wrenched out the lance and dove clear as the whale lurched crazily forward under the drive of his single fluke. The canoe was with him at once and Hagilt and Hinak hauled him back aboard.

The whale had rolled completely over, showing the white underside of his flukes and flippers and the coarse white grooves of his throat and chest. Tokwit said quietly: "You have done what you wanted, Hawil. Tell us what to do with him."

From the other canoe Kon-gass asked: "Is it a gift to shame Eskowit, Hawil?"

"No," answered Atlin. "To make him great."

"Will you ask him for Watsika?" Hagilt asked.

"No," answered Atlin again. "We give it as his right and ask nothing in return."

"How can that be?" asked the fifth paddler. "When you killed him yourself and brought him here?"

"Be quiet and listen," someone told him. "A great chief is speaking. What do you know of the ways of chiefs?"

Atlin pointed to the shoreline. "The current is carrying us into the Tsitikath waters. We must arrange the whale for towing, with his mouth closed and the floats close about him. Then we will tie our canoes to him and paddle towards our own village. But we will paddle only hard enough to steer the whale towards shore while it is drifting northward in the current."

There was a murmur of excitement and approval from the crews. Every man seemed to follow the complicated meaning of Atlin's words and to understand that he was taking part in something that would last forever in the history of the tribes. The canoes moved in on the whale and the work of securing him for towing began.

The northward drift was strong. By the time they were ready to tow they were in sight of the Tsitikat village and several canoes had already put off. Atlin brought Tokwit to the bow to stand by him and speak for him; Hagilt moved to the stern to steer. He set a course that angled across the current, carrying the whale steadily towards shore and nearer to the village. "I am glad you do not want us to take this one home, Hawil," he said. "Our hands would never come free of the paddles again."

The first of the Tsitikat canoes were close now. Atlin recognised Tsitlas, the war chief, standing in the bow of the nearest. "Ho, you Hotsath men," Tsitlas shouted. "The Chief of the Tsitikat sends to know what it is you take from his waters."

"Tell the Chief it is a whale," answered Tokwit. "It is caught

in his power and will not come with us. Tell him he had better come quickly before we let it go."

"Is it a trick, that you do not paddle harder?" asked Tsitlas.

"It is no trick," answered Tokwit. "But it is too hard for you to understand. Better hurry and tell your Chief, because this is an affair of great chiefs."

They were quite close to the village now and many more canoes had come out. At last Atlin saw Eskowit, standing with his speaker at the bow of one of his great freight canoes. If they were close to the village they were also, Tokwit and Atlin well knew, close to the eddy behind Hotsath Island that would take them back into their own waters. It was clear that Eskowit knew this also. His speaker asked them: "The Chief would know why you have come into his waters. What is it that you have and cannot control?"

"My Chief tells you that a great dead whale has brought him here," answered Tokwit. "It is caught in your Chief's power, as the sea lion was long ago. If your Chief is ready to take it, we will let it go."

The speaker consulted with Eskowit, then turned to them again. "The Chief asks why you have not towed the whale away. If you are weak and cannot tow it, why do you not let it go and leave our waters?"

All the people in the canoes understood the meaning of the wordy struggle and waited eagerly for each new phase of it. Tokwit answered: "We have towed and towed, but some power is holding it back. That is why my Chief has called for your Chief. But he cannot let the whale go unless your Chief will take it and your people will welcome it and honour it. If he did otherwise he would offend the Whale Spirit."

These words gave the key to the whole matter. The canoes drew closer and the people were talking back and forth among themselves while Eskowit's speaker again consulted with him. If Eskowit accepted the whale he would be under obligation to

Atlin, no matter what was said. At last the speaker turned to
them again: "The Chief would know what it is the Hotsath
Chief expects of him. There is a matter between them that is
not settled."

Tokwit answered at once: "Only that he take the whale in
place of the sea lion and that he and his people honour it by
singing and dancing, that they sprinkle it with swansdown and
eagle down and welcome it as a guest to their village."

In one of the Tsitikat canoes a single voice began a song
of welcome. It was joined by other voices and soon all the
Tsitikats were singing softly and rhythmically.

Eskowit's speaker stood forward and raised his voice again:
"When you release the whale the Tsitikat Chief will take it.
The people have begun to sing already. They will welcome it
and honour it as it should be honoured."

The whaling crews stopped paddling and began to haul on
the tow lines to release the whale. Tokwit spoke again: "My
Chief asks if you will return the harpoon heads to him when you
cut them out. They are yours because they have drifted to you
with the whale, but he values them greatly and would like to
have them."

Eskowit spoke directly in answer: "Tell your Chief I will send
him the harpoon heads and the lines and the floats. I know well
he could have cut them out himself if he had wished. Tell him
also to send his sea otter robe to me again. I have seen it only
twice. That is not enough to understand its beauty."

Tokwit answered: "The Chief will send it very soon. He
says: Let the Tsitikat Chief keep it long enough this time to
understand its beauty."

It was dusk and the south wind was rising as the Tsitikat
canoes took the whale in tow and turned for their village. The
two Hotsath canoes turned into the eddy of Hotsath Island and
swung towards the channel behind it that would take them
home. Many of the Tsitikat canoes followed with them at

first, still singing their welcome to the whale. The people in the Hotsath canoes jokingly began a wedding song, calling on Atlin to join them. While they were still singing he turned to Hinak.

"You heard the words, my brother," he said. "Many of them were yours. One day you shall be my speaker."

"You have made many difficult things true, Hawil," answered Hinak. "I believe this also."

Atlin settled into his place and listened to the talk and singing of the paddlers behind him. His right hand reached out and felt the smooth wood of the new harpoon shaft, which showed its golden colour faintly in the fading light. But his mind was counting time, the time it would take to send the sea otter robe to Eskowit again and receive his answer.